Hollow Blood

The Hunt for the Foul Murderer of Ichabod Crane

Sleepy Hollow Horrors: Book One

AUSTIN DRAGON

This is a work of fiction. Names, characters, places, and incidents are the product of the author's imagination or are used fictitiously. Any resemblance to actual persons, living or dead, events, or locales is entirely coincidental.

Copyright © 2015 by Austin Dragon

All rights reserved. No part of this publication may be reproduced, distributed, or transmitted in any form or by any means, or stored in a database or retrieval system, without the prior written permission of the publisher.

Published by Well-Tailored Books, California

Hollow Blood / Sleepy Hollow Horrors (Book 1)

978-0-9909315-2-2 (hardcover)
978-0-9909315-1-5 (paperback)
978-0-9909315-0-8 (ebook)

http://www.austindragon.com

Book cover design by Whendell Souza

Formatting by Polgarus Studio

Printed in the United States of America

Contents

Introduction 1

Part I: BROM BONES 3
    Poor, Unfortunate Ichabod 5
    The Hunter 6
    What Remains 16
    Sleepy Hollow Boys 25
    Vengeance 35
    Trouble 47
    Warpath 60
    Showdown 73
    Follow 86

Part II: THE MARSHAL 95
    Omen 97
    Trek 104
    Detour 114
    Distant Shadow 124
    Bounty Hunters 134
    Wagon Train 146
    About Marshal 157
    The Storm 179
    Psycho 189

Part III: THE HESSIAN 199
    Ride! Across the Bridge From Hell! 201

Introduction

My part in this horrific affair began five years ago. My parents had learned of the death, indirectly through third parties, two years after the original event in, of all things, a ghost story, and inquired further. When I became aware of the tragedy, I took the inquiries upon myself until I came to know a man named Diedrich Knickerbocker. It was his last post, in our nearly one year correspondence, that not only gave the fullest account of the alleged circumstances of the original event, but also the surrounding background and details. It was that letter that precipitated my quest, which, unsurprisingly to all who know me, evolved into my current situation.

In the late autumn of 1790, Ichabod Crane, a well-likeable schoolmaster in the New England town of Sleepy Hollow, disappeared in body from the face of God's Earth. Folks say in whispers what they refused to say aloud — he was 'taken' by the chief spirit that haunted the Hollow — the Headless Horseman.

Aye, this Headless Horseman. Some say, this horseman was bewitched by a German warlock in the earliest days of colonial settlement. Some say, an ancient Indian chieftain and sorcerer held dark pow-wows on the very land that is the Hollow. The Horseman, who, as legend has it, had his head carried away by a cannonball in the War, haunted the Hollow's valley in his nightly quest for his head. This Horseman is a giant of a man—albeit headless—in black clothes and a massive cloak, sitting on a fearsome black horse. This Horseman chases his unfortunate mortal victim, rising in his stirrups to throw its dreadful pumpkin, then passes by like a whirlwind, and disappears into the night.

Aye, they would declare, the Headless Horseman of Sleepy Hollow.

I, however, believe in no such feeble supernatural tales, though the simple people of Sleepy Hollow regard them as unimpeachable certainties. However, the murder of a man, in all my considerable experience despite my youth in age, remains the province of other men of flesh and blood, and not ghosts and boogiemen. The Foul Murderer of Ichabod Crane is whom I seek. And when I find this man, without any hesitation to burden myself with any civilized reflections or academic considerations in 'seeking justice and not revenge,' all irrelevant to my purpose and irrelevant to my hunt, I shall kill this devil.

Part I

Brom Bones

Poor, Unfortunate Ichabod

"Death by another name."

His very eyes bulged from their sockets. His teeth jutted forward from his wide-open mouth, unable to scream. His ponytail flew and flapped behind his head, and his hands clutched his horse, Gunpowder, with inhuman strength borne out of the depths of panic.

Ichabod rode the horse out of Sleepy Hollow in the grips of incredible terror. The ground was ripped up with the terrible force of his horror-stricken horse as both man and beast disappeared into the night.

In close pursuit, the black goblin horse appeared with its huge, misshapen, towering rider—a glowing pumpkin already in the rider's hand. The rider had neither neck nor head on his shoulders. They raced after their prey like an unstoppable force.

It was a fall day in 1790, and it was Ichabod Crane's last night—last day—alive.

The Hunter

> *"To blame the foul murder of a good man on an imaginary apparition may be the way of the superstitious folk of these sleepy country-sides, but my vengeance upon his true murderer shall not be denied."*

This was the place of ghosts, banshees, creeping shadows…and the Legend.

Sleepy Hollow seemed like most of the towns nestled away in spacious coves that dotted the eastern shore of the Hudson River. This region was settled by the descendants of Dutch voyagers who came in search of the New World. It was, as its name suggested, a peaceful, valley glen, however, it was different from all the others in that it was home to the most enduring and frightening of the region's supernatural tales. The land itself had a quality of unnatural influence in the air that made the imaginations of the average person, even the most skeptical one, see and hear things that were not truly there.

A young man continued his slow ride into town, his mind wandering. "I may be here when you get back," she had said to him those many, many months back when he set his mind to his "hunt." "Maybe."

The woman who was supposed to be his wife glanced at him once more before she climbed into her awaiting carriage and left him behind, standing alone on a New Haven, Connecticut street. She was right to be vexed with him. He was a man obsessed, and no other life for him would be possible until he brought the affair to its final end.

He thought of her often at the beginning, but as he made his way up the Hudson Valley, ever closer to Sleepy Hollow, all his mind concerned itself with was the confrontation with that "foul murderer." Now after his long journey, his destination was a mere minute away on horseback.

This New England autumn day was without the previous day's cold winds. A nice breeze blew through the trees that covered the glen with their beautiful yellow and brown leaves. Upon a pointed grassy knoll, one of many in these parts, a youngish man in a worn, out-of-fashion, three-cornered hat sat on a large and graceful horse. The animal's coat was a shiny shade of black, save for a white streak down its forehead. Both were so still that they could have been mistaken for statues. His face had an expression of hardened determination as he scanned the land slowly, moving his head only slightly. He imagined being here, on this very spot, when lying awake on restless nights, impatient, contemplating, and dreaming about finally arriving. Now, at long last, Sleepy Hollow was before him.

Despite its haunted reputation far and wide, he believed none of it, whether this region or any other, with all manner of indigenous frightening and fantastical legends to match. The stories about these parts were endless. He had a personal disdain for any man who let his life be governed by fanciful superstitions, even the Indian whose customs were intertwined with such beliefs. Men were supposed to grow out of such folly, not spread their tall tales by spoken and written word to every corner of the land. Most times it could be ignored by the rational man, but occasionally these imaginings could seize grown townspeople with such frenzy that only terrible outcomes could result, as was shown centuries ago with the event of the Salem Witch Trials in old colonial Massachusetts — innocents killed by the law on the testimony, the lies, of a group of little girls. However, even in modern 1800, centuries later, stories of ghosts and evil things roaming about in the night persisted.

Even he had to admit to himself that, as he and his horse, Caleb Williams, neared this place, there was something unnatural about it. It was a feeling that he couldn't shake from his mind or body. It was a feeling that he couldn't quite put into words, but it was as tangible and consequential as any solid object of substance he had ever come across. It was an ominous calmness, waiting for something bad to manifest. He took comfort in knowing — or convinced himself — that he was that badness coming to happen.

But it was not all imagination. There were actual manifestations that he had encountered during the journey. He had come across more than one wild animal — a black bird, something swimming in the stream, maybe some species of water snake — all gazing upon him with devilish eyes, all acting more like the scheming imps of fables than the normal fauna of nature. It was common on a long journey to imagine the trees, dark in the night, to be inanimate sentinels, spying on your every move. The only time that imagination became much more was when a hellish wolf took to howling at the moon in a ferocious manner, not more than ten feet from where they had situated themselves to make camp. After the commotion, he had his gun at the ready, but the beast seemed to disappear.

Even today, there was another *occurrence*. Down a desolate path, they came across a puddle of blood. Some kind of animal, a rabbit perhaps, had been killed and whisked away, but the brightness of the red and amount of blood was unnatural. His horse didn't need any prompting. He instinctively moved off the road and into the brush so as not to have to step near the blood puddle. Julian put it out of his mind.

Many long months and many lonely miles of travel finally brought him here, a journey spurred by the receipt of a plain, crinkled piece of paper. His eyes locked on his final destination now before him—the reclusive glen of Sleepy Hollow.

"*It be the quietest, sleepiest, place in the whole world.*" He remembered the words of some townsman he had come across days ago, back in the nearby town of Sing Sing. But it wasn't quiet, at least not at this moment. Birdsong filled the air—almost suddenly it seemed to him. The October air was nippy but not uncomfortable. Along the shores of the Atlantic, such towns were not exclusive to the Hudson. Every state had its own imitations secluded away. He probably ran through most of them when he was attached to General Washington, chasing after or running from Redcoats in the War. He may not have been a man-soldier then, but he was a soldier, nevertheless—a drummer boy for the American Continental Army. The War freed him from the doldrums of the schoolhouse and the awful Mrs. 'Beetle-face.' Even being a child, he conducted himself like a real soldier, even if he was too small to carry a musket, let alone shoot one.

But he could shoot one now, and kill a man, too.

"We go, Caleb Williams," he said quietly as he gave his horse's reins a firm tug, accompanied by a firm kick with the heel of his right foot. The animal moved forward.

He paused at the door of the quaint home. There was no mirror for him to gaze at himself, but he ran his hand down the front of his chest, checked his buttons, looked down at his shoes, touched his dark hat on his head, and touched the sides of his dark brown hair. His supposed-to-be-wife was right. Menfolk fuss over themselves every bit as much as womenfolk. They just hide themselves, even from other men, when they do. The day before in Tarry Town, he did manage to stop for a good shave to properly trim his mustache and beard, so he was confident in his professional appearance. He said it to himself clearly in his mind. All the planning, journeying, contemplating every step, move and countermove in his mind, it had all come to this.

It all begins with this friendly knock on this door.

"Call me Julian, ma'am." He smiled a big smile as he tipped his three-cornered hat and bowed his head to the woman in a long fluid motion before firmly placing it back on his slicked-backed black hair. "I am here to chase away the doldrums and even those minor dark moods and darker spirits, with my genial disposition and learned repartee."

The buxom woman laughed at the young man with his constantly moving frame. He was tall and lean, but with strong shoulders, more muscle than bone, and the slightly callused hands of a man of toil rather than leisure, despite his fancy dress.

"You're a funny soul," she said. "What might your surname be?" The middle-aged woman was short and round, wearing a dark blue work dress, and her head and neck wrapped with a shawl. She leaned against the open door frame with her arms folded.

"My dear ma'am, are we not long, lost kindred confidants who have left such formalities behind eons ago?"

She laughed again. "*Eons?* I'm not all that up in years, and you are barely past being a youngin' on your father's lap. What are you trying to sell me, stranger? Because you are not from these parts. Be cautious on how you answer, because right now you have my interest. In a moment, you shall have my door slammed shut in your face."

Julian laughed. "I'm fond of a woman who declares her state of mind plainly."

"I'm sure you are fond of other things when it comes to a woman, but out with your intentions, Julian with no last name."

Julian straightened himself and seemed to grow an inch or two. He reached into his jacket for a small, brown leather notepad with a tiny pencil between its pages.

"Ma'am, I am in search of one Ichabod Crane."

The woman's smile disappeared from her face. "I don't know who that is, stranger." She began closing the door, but Julian leaned forward with an outstretched hand.

"Please ma'am. There is no call for little falsehoods. I may have to speak with many of the good townspeople of Sleepy Hollow, but all I need is for one fine soul to assist me in my quest. My employers have directed me to locate and converse with one Ichabod Crane, and I am authorized to handsomely compensate any kind person who assists me in this most important task."

"Compensate?" she asked, her disposition instantly reverted back to cordial.

"Handsomely." Julian smiled. "And we don't even have to tell your husband."

The woman's smile also returned.

The home of Mrs. Mulder was as cozy and quaint as the one of Mrs. Van Boor, only this one still clamored with small children, the oldest of which was no more than ten.

"Tell me about Mr. Ichabod Crane?" Julian asked as he sat at the family table, poised with his pencil and small notepad.

"Ichabod...there is so much to recall, but all of it good. I believe he was Connecticut-born. Not sure what he did there exactly, but here in the Hollow, he was our chief schoolmaster. Yes, 'spare the rod and spoil the child,' he always said. He would do his duty by their parents. He kept a firm hand on the urchins, but his punishments were never vindictive or arbitrary. He always helped the little children and never gave the big children more than they could handle. He had a soft heart. He would even play with the larger boys in the fields and chaperon the little boys to their homes. 'Who knows what shades and spirits could be lurking?' he would say.

"Everyone here sure enjoyed seeing him, especially the

womenfolk. From house-to-house he'd go, bringing all the accounts of the day, all the good gossip." She suddenly burst out with a laugh. A funny image had obviously popped into her mind. "That man could eat! He had the appetite of a jungle lion but nowhere could you see where the food went. He was so tall and skinny. Skinny shoulders, with long arms and long legs dangling about, far out of his clothes. We sometimes called him Daddy-Long-Limbs." She laughed again. "I sure do miss that smiling face, with those huge ears sitting on that skinny neck of his and his bobbin' Adam's apple."

Julian smiled. The woman had a genuine affection for Ichabod even after these long ten years.

"Yes, everyone was fond of Ichabod." She smiled, teary-eyed.

"Is that a fact?" a voice called out.

A large man stood at the doorway, removing his black felt hat from his head. His sweaty face showed obvious anger as he stared at Julian. "Who are you, and what are you doing in my house with my wife and children?"

Julian stood to attention and stepped forward. The wife was already scolding her husband to be more hospitable. "Call me Julian, sir." He vigorously shook Mr. Mulder's hand. "I am here on behalf of the Estate of J, period, Doyle Senior."

"Estate?" The husband looked at him with confusion.

"Yes, sir. I have been directed to locate Mr. Ichabod Crane for the purposes of settling the Estate of J. Doyle Senior of New Haven, Connecticut. I have also been authorized to handsomely compensate any person or persons whom can lead me to Mr. Ichabod Crane."

The husband thought for a moment. "Ichabod Crane?"

He looked at his wife. "Isn't he the one—?"

Mrs. Mulder quickly interrupted him. "I was telling Julian about Ichabod, but perhaps he should repeat the details of the compensation from this estate." She motioned to her husband to join them at the table, and he shifted his large bottom on the wooden chair to get comfortable.

"Is this reward...would it be dispersed...whether Mr. Ichabod Crane was found to be alive or...dead?" he asked.

Julian nodded. "Yes, sir, absolutely. The compensation or, if you prefer, reward, would be dispersed whether the heir was found alive or deceased, to any person who assisted in determining the exact whereabouts of the heir. The point is that the disposition of the heir has to be determined in good time, rather than drag out the process over months or years. Time is money."

"How much is this reward?" the husband asked.

"You would have almost as many shiny coins to rub together as a man in these parts called... Brom Bones. I heard that if there were any person who could be called the best compatriot of Mr. Ichabod Crane, that person would be Brom Bones. Do you know where he currently resides?"

"Best compatriot?" Mrs. Mulder looked puzzled and glanced at her husband. "Brom Bones was the living tormenting terror of poor Ichabod."

Mr. Mulder stood from his chair, his brow wrinkled with suspicion. "Are you looking for Ichabod Crane or Brom Bones?"

"And Katrina Van Tassel too, sir. All of Mr. Ichabod Crane's good acquaintances." He laughed. "I was told that Mr. Ichabod Crane planned to marry that fine woman."

"Katrina Van Brunt," Mr. Mulder corrected.

"Van Brunt?" Julian asked.

"Yes. Mrs. Van Brunt," Mr. Mulder said again. "She married a decade ago."

Julian committed the new fact to memory. "Then I would very much like to speak with both her and her husband."

The Mulders glanced at each other again, before turning back to Julian.

"You don't know do you?" Mr. Mulder pointed out. "You must have forgotten to put it in that little book of yours that you carry around. Bones, as in Brom Bones, is a nickname; it is not his family name. It's Van Brunt. It's Mr. and Mrs. Brom and Katrina Van Brunt."

Julian's smile disappeared.

I have the motive for the murder!

What Remains

*"All that he was, all that he would be,
this is all that remains in this world of the man."*

Julian kicked a rock and watched it roll down the slanted ground. Caleb Williams briefly raised his head to watch but returned to his grazing. The decaying schoolhouse that was once the benevolent kingdom of Ichabod Crane sat in total solitude and decay on the hill. Only three of its four log walls remained, and cobwebs hung thick throughout the structure from top to bottom. The wood had a sickening rot. Some parts looked moist, and others bone-dry. The ground inside was matted with weeds and every other kind of noxious plant. The glass of the windows was long gone, with only jagged shards remaining. Julian looked up and observed an empty bird's nest under a section of the roof that had not fallen away.

"Why doesn't the town tear down this unsightly edifice?" Julian asked.

The old-timer stood with his hand firmly grasping his suspenders at the chest. "It's haunted of course. That's why." He chewed his pipe as he smoked.

Mr. Berg had a bushy beard, but no mustache. A dark brown hat covered his leathery face and his coat, breeches, stockings, and shoes all were in matching shades of brown.

"Haunted by whom?" Julian asked the old-timer.

"The usual spirits that wander these parts of the Hollow."

"This is the nineteenth century, not the ninth," Julian said bitterly under his breath.

Berg inhaled on his pipe again. "You got a mean streak in ya, don't you?"

"I'm sorry, sir. It's this place. It's set me off in a bad disposition. I read the accounts of it before I arrived. A happy schoolhouse brimming with noisy but bright children. A justifiable pride for the people of the town. And today, to see this…rotting shack that remains."

The old-timer nodded and cast his gaze at the structure again. "Yes, it is a shame. But don't fret. If the town doesn't get to it, the land will rightly reclaim it so no one will ever know there was anything on this ground. All the town's children go for schooling in Tarry Town nowadays. They got a brand-new, fancy schoolhouse there."

"Saw it on the ride in."

"There's been quite a few changes since the time of Mr. Ichabod Crane. We also got ourselves a new church in Tarry Town, too. Wiley's swamp was drained away and plenty more folks movin' in, but they mostly are settled in Tarry Town. The Hollow is for us original settlers."

"Was Mr. Ichabod Crane only a schoolmaster for the Hollow?"

"Oh, no. Schooling children gave him only a meager salary. You have to be in the bigger towns and cities for that. He helped local farmers with light work, such as fence-mendin', cuttin' wood, takin' the animals to water and pasture. He had no wife or kin, just set up nightly domicile in the barn of one of the town farmers. He also excelled as a singing master, teaching the psalms. He made good wages that way. I always remembered him singing at church. His voice would carry above the entire congregation."

"Mr. Ichabod Crane, Jack-of-all-trades."

"Who are you again, mister?"

"I told you already."

"You told me something."

"Can you point me to the Van Brunt residence?"

"No." The old-timer shook his head as he smiled with his pipe held between his teeth.

"Why not?"

"You're trouble, mister. Get on your black horse and ride back to where you came from."

"If I did that, I'd deprive you good people of some decent gossip. But thanks anyway, sir. I'll just ride until I find the biggest home in the Hollow. I'm sure that will be Van Brunt residence."

The elderly man smiled as he took his pipe from mouth. He looked at it and then put it back to hang from his lips. "I have a feeling I'll be seeing you again."

"I doubt that."

"I'm the undertaker, mister. I'll be seeing everyone at some time."

"Unless some undertaker has the pleasure of seeing you first."

The man looked back at him and smirked. Julian turned to walk back to his horse and grabbed the reins as he effortlessly mounted. He rode back to the man.

"Here's what I promised, sir." Julian leaned down from the saddle and handed the man a few bits of coin.

"Thank you, mister. I enjoyed answering the questions that you already knew."

Julian smiled and said, "Be wary of ghosts, undertakers...and ghostly undertakers."

The old-timer laughed. Julian touched the tip of his hat as he turned and galloped away.

Hans Van Ripper stood at the open door, staring at him with a highly irritated expression and a slightly jutting jaw. He was an old man with gray hair, eyebrows, mustache, and beard in dirty clothes from some kind of work in the field.

"Good day, sir. I was told to call on you by local townspeople. I am Julian, and I am in the employ of the Estate of J. Doyle Senior to find the exact whereabouts of one Ichabod Crane for purposes of settling all affairs related to the disposition of an inheritance."

"He's dead, mister. Ten years ago." Van Ripper's voice was straightforward and curt.

"How do you know that, sir?" Julian asked.

The man had already begun to close his front door but stopped at the question. He considered Julian for a moment. "Please sir, I shall compensate you for your time."

"Come on in," Van Ripper said as he backed away from the entrance to allow Julian to enter. "Please sit." Van Ripper motioned to an empty chair.

It was a warm cabin and filled with clutter. An oversized supper table, a few chairs in front of the main stone fireplace, and a wide four-shelf bookcase leaning against the walls, which was so inundated with books, papers, and knickknacks that it seemed in danger of falling over any minute. Julian could see the kitchen in the corner, one open door in the back (obviously the bedroom) and a closed door in the back (must be to outside).

"You were saying that Mr. Ichabod Crane is dead. How are you certain of that, sir?"

"Everybody knows that. He was taken."

"Taken?"

"By the Horseman."

"You don't truly believe in that legend?" Julian's face showed his annoyance.

"Ichabod was taken by the Headless Horseman. All that was left of him that night was his hat and a shattered pumpkin on the road to the church. That was all. That and all his possessions that he kept in a handkerchief at whatever home or barn or shed he resided in at the moment. He had no other possessions in the world. The night after the event all the town's boys showed up at schoolhouse as normal, but Ichabod was no place to be seen. Ichabod was never absent or tardy. If he didn't show, that meant he was sick or dead. And he wasn't sick. Lunchtime came, suppertime came, late night, and no Ichabod, nor the next day or next. Ichabod's dead, mister. Ten years since."

"Was there a body?"

"Demon spirits don't leave your body behind. They take you and there's nothing to be found of you."

"Mr. Van Ripper…" Julian hesitated for a moment. He had to pose his next words as carefully as possible as to not offend. "My employers need some kind of tangible proof of death. They can't go before authorities and state Mr. Ichabod Crane as dead with no remains whatsoever because a ghost took him. Did anyone see…the event?"

"Absolutely, not. If you want to remain among the living."

"Have you ever seen this Headless Horseman?"

"I'm alive, ain't I? I'm sitting in front of you, ain't I? Absolutely, not. And I pray I never do."

"Why are you and the people of Sleepy Hollow so convinced that Mr. Ichabod Crane is dead then? Did you search for him?"

Van Ripper smiled. "We searched high and low for him. The brook, all roads, the old churchyard, and the entire valley. We searched even places the Horseman never went. We even drained Wiley's Swamp to be sure Ichabod had not fallen and drowned there."

"You said all that was left besides his hat was a pumpkin?"

"Yes."

"From the Horseman?"

"Yes."

"A ghostly horseman, riding a ghostly horse, but leaves behind a tangible pumpkin that any mortal man, woman, or child could see, touch, and pick up."

Van Ripper thought for a moment.

"Mr. Van Ripper, I submit to you that some mischievous person or persons played a terrible act of deception on you and the good people of Sleepy Hollow. Got you and the people to believe that the Horseman did away with Ichabod and scared poor Ichabod out of his mind. He probably started running and never stopped until he was a few states away."

"Sounds plausible, mister. Several people have said the very same thing. A few even said they've seen him in northern part of the state a few years back. Very plausible, except for one thing."

"What's that?"

Van Ripper rose from his chair and grabbed something from the top of a bookshelf. He walked over and placed the book in front of Julian, *Cotton Mather's History of Witchcraft*. "Ichabod would never have left without this. Even if he had to walk all the way back from whatever place he got to, no matter how far. I knew Ichabod well, and he was superstitious down to his bones. If the house was on fire, he'd even grab this book before he'd grab the Good Book."

"Do you remember all the possessions he left behind?"

"Know them by heart, this book, the King James Bible, the New England Almanac, two shirts, two socks." Van Ripper sat back down at the table. "Two pair of stockings, pair of clothes, corduroy, razor, broken pipe, book of the psalms, and a book of dreams and fortune-tellin'."

"How can you be so accurate in your recollection? It was ten years ago."

Van Ripper pointed to the bookshelf. "Because I see them every day, all of it on top of that bookshelf in a bowl. He was a bachelor and had no kin to claim it. I would be the closest I guess. I am the executor of his estate." He laughed. "Which means all his knickknacks went to me. What if you can't corroborate his death?"

"Then my work is done. But again, I believe there to be a natural rather than supernatural explanation for his disappearance."

"Or death."

"Or death."

"I don't know how you would prove it either way. For my part, and most of the people of the Hollow, it was the Horseman. I would swear to it."

"Even though you never saw the Horseman yourself."

"I've never seen your brain either, but I'd swear you have one with all the thinkin' going on in that skull of yours." Van Ripper stood from the table. "There was one other thing that dear Ichabod left behind from that night." He walked across to a side window, and Julian joined him. "There." Van Ripper was pointing.

"What am I looking at?" Julian asked.

"The grave."

Julian now focused his gaze on the barely noticeable raised mound of earth nearly fifteen yards from the house.

"Who?"

"Not a who. Gunpowder, my late horse. I lent it to Ichabod that night. He was off to a big evening party at Old Baltus Van Tassel's, along with my most expensive possession still—my saddle. We found the saddle on the same road leading to church, in the dirt, trampled by the horse. Ichabod's hat and the pumpkin were found near the brook, beyond the old bridge."

"They both disappeared?"

Van Ripper tapped on the glass of the window to point again at the grave outside and continued. "The horse was found the next morning, but he was not right in the head. His hoof tracks were found deeply dented into the road from obviously running away at such a furious speed. It's no wonder his legs didn't fly off. A couple of nights later, Gunpowder ran off. He never had done that before. I believe my horse saw the Horseman again on his nightly quest for his lost head and ran in terror from it. Gunpowder returned home a month later. He was always a lanky horse. You could always see his ribs on the sides. He was blind in one eye too, but he was a fit animal, despite his frame, and despite his years. He was not that way that day. He was sickly. Deathlike. He was covered in bloody sores that just seemed to bleed for no reason. The poor animal had stumbled back from whatever hell it escaped from and carried itself with whatever will it had left and died right there on that spot. Gunpowder was like my kin, so I buried him like he was such. I didn't even need to get help to drag the body into the grave. His body was that light. It had shriveled away. It's been almost ten years later and nothing will grow on that spot. Nothing."

Julian looked at the horse's grave again.

"I knew Ichabod a long time, mister. I knew my horse a longer time. My horse ran away from something with such terror that it journeyed, God only knows how many miles away, and then reversed to get back home. My poor old horse collapsed and died right at my feet. No mortal man could have put that terror in my horse. None. It was the Horseman, I tell you. It killed Ichabod, and the sight of it again killed my horse. Do some thinkin' on that, mister."

Sleepy Hollow Boys

*"Leave the matter of this man,
long-gone, alone — or you will join him."*

A black hat on his head and a thick coat over his body, the man spied on the Van Ripper cabin from the hill. He was not at all visible, unless one knew he was there, straddling his horse but keeping his profile hidden among the trees.

Word had already begun to spread throughout the Hollow about the "Inheritance Man" looking for Ichabod Crane. That's how it was in small towns. Someone had news to tell and they told it, even if they had to run to the next neighbor's house. And that person would do the same. More than a few were suspicious of the stranger and his true motives. Why would anyone be looking for Ichabod Crane after a decade?

He was the closest sentry. The other two men were at their posts within eyeshot. There was only one main road from Tarry Town through Sleepy Hollow, and strangers never strayed from it. Their plan was simple — wait for him to come to them.

Out of habit, he pulled his pocket watch and flipped it

open. The time was no matter because they were to stay here in wait until the stranger came out of the cabin and follow him close. It was now two hours since he had entered.

What could that old mutt Van Ripper and he have to talk about for so long?

He saw the main cabin door open.

His head tilted around the tree to get a better view. There was Van Ripper walking from his porch to the side of his cabin to start cutting the logs into more wood for the fireplace, an odd thing to do with strange company in the house. He watched for a few moments, then longer. Van Ripper continued his work, in no hurry at all, and no one exited the cabin.

Van Ripper was now into a good rhythm. Quick forceful swings and he was able to cut the wood into manageable pieces in no more than two cuts. He heard noise and stopped to look up to see Ayden riding down to him on his brown horse.

"Good day, Hans."

Van Ripper held his ax with one hand, resting it on his shoulder. "What brings you around, Ayden?"

"I was lookin' for that stranger. The Inheritance Man. I was told he was by you."

"Wait!"

Hans was not looking at Ayden but off to some nearby trees. The ax dropped to the ground and the old man suddenly had a gun in his hand. He fired. All Ayden saw was an animal moving away and its head explode.

"You got a bloody mess there, Hans. There'll be nothing left of that hare for you to eat."

"They usually don't come so close and just sit there for

you to shoot at. What do you want again?"

"Where's the stranger who was here by you?"

"He left almost…two hours ago."

Ayden was taken aback and looked around. "Where'd he go?"

"Out the back door of my place. He said he was being followed."

Ayden was flustered and looked out to the woods behind the cabin. "Damn."

"Seems he was right."

"Where was he goin', Hans? Mr. Van Brunt will be angry with us for losin' him. Where'd he go?"

"I don't know where he went."

"Hans, we'll be back to deal with you." Ayden quickly rode past him to the woods behind the cabin.

"Ayden, don't come back to my land! If Brom wants to talk to me, then he better do it himself and not send no Sleepy Hollow Boys to my land again!"

Ayden ignored Van Ripper's yelling as he looked at the ground for any signs of the stranger's horse. He stopped and rode the horse side to side, then zigzagged around, and finally galloped forward just a few paces at a time.

He jumped down from his horse and bent down to scan the ground. His horse tried to move away, but he held the reins tight. He looked forward at the horizon and then scanned it from left to right.

Ayden squinted and then stood on his tiptoes. "What's that?"

He could see someone on a horse in the distance. It was only a silhouette, but it was clear to him that whoever it was, they were watching him too.

"Ayden!"

He looked behind him to see the two other horsemen riding up.

"Ayden, what are you doing? Where's that man?" Ace yelled at him.

Both men were similarly dressed. Ace looked to be the oldest of the three. The third man looked like a boy, but he was older than both men.

"He snuck out the back way of Hans' cabin. I think I found him though—" Ayden whipped back around, but the silhouette was gone. "Damn. Where'd he go again?"

"Where? You had him in your sights?"

"Yes, but he's gone again."

"Get on your horse then and let's go!"

Ayden clumsily mounted his horse and settled back on the saddle. His body jerked up, startled.

A pumpkin smashed to the ground in the center of the three men. The men jumped, and one of the horses rose up on two legs and almost threw Ace off.

Julian galloped to the men.

Ace yelled, "That was a damn thing to do, mister. Why did you do that?"

Julian reached them, but stopped a few paces back. "I don't like to be followed by horse thieves."

"We're no horse thieves, mister," Ayden said.

"Who are you then?"

"Never you mind who we are, mister. We live in this town and you don't," Ace snapped.

"What's the penalty for horse thieves in these parts?" Julian now revealed a rifle trained on them, resting just above his thigh.

"Mister, we are no horse thieves. There's no need for any violence here. This is all a misunderstanding."

"Get down from your horses."

The men dismounted one by one. Ace said, "Mister, just remain calm. We're doing as you say."

"Hand me the reins," Julian commanded.

Ace started to move.

"No! You do it." Julian pointed at Ayden with his rifle.

Ayden handed him the reins of all three horses. Julian dismounted from his horse, but kept his rifle trained on them. He wrapped the reins to the back of the saddle of his horse.

"What are you plannin' on doin,' mister?" Alfie, the third man, asked.

Julian got back on his horse. "I am leaving you here to walk awhile and consider your actions to this point in your life, and for you to decide how you want to proceed in your life after I ride away."

Julian suddenly jumped down and walked to them.

"Mister, no violence!" Ace held up his hands as Julian pointed his rifle. "We did what you said."

"Did you fight in the War?"

Ace hesitated. "What kind of question is that? Every able-bodied man in these parts did. There are no yellow-bellies here in the Hollow."

"Which side?"

Ace laughed. "The side of America. No Tories any place here or beyond the Hollow you could get to by foot or by horse."

Julian nodded. "My story, too." He lowered his rifle. "I'll let you keep your firearms then. No ex-soldier with the honor and courage of fighting for these United States of America is capable of a cowardly act, let alone anything as low as shooting a fellow ex-soldier in the back as he rides away."

Julian mounted his horse again and galloped away with the three men's horses in tow.

Ace pulled his gun from his back waist. The other two men looked at him as he aimed to shoot. They all glanced at each other, and Ace stopped himself. "Damn!"

"What do we do now?" Ayden asked with a hint of panic in his voice. "I think it would have been better if he did shoot us."

Abraham Van Brunt was still known by all, save strangers, as Brom Bones. But call him anything but "Mr. Van Brunt" at your peril. He was a burly, broad-shouldered, handsome man with short, curly black hair and a full beard and mustache. He was often impatiently barking orders at his men for one thing or another. It was not the days of his youth when there was always an air of fun about him just under the surface. With his high status now, he expected near-perfection in his business and on his land. Maybe he was an arrogant taskmaster nowadays, but the word he preferred was confident. He knew what he wanted, and he wanted nothing less than that.

Before he became the master of this estate, he was already a hero of the Hollow, known for his exploits of strength and daring—and mischief. He left that all behind and was now the wealthiest man in the region with all the power and prestige that came with such status.

He stood in his field clothes—still fancy dress to any outsider who might see him—on the porch of his "castle"—the largest residence in all of Sleepy Hollow, Tarry Town and all neighboring townships.

The Van Brunt place was almost as large as a township

itself. The outermost marker of his property was a giant elm tree. All of his land was impressive. The wild parts were filled with all manner of birds—martins, swallows, and others—nesting in the lush trees, and the snow geese spent their time in the great pond nearby. The tended parts, behind the wooden fences, had pigs, goats, guinea fowl, turkey, and chickens roaming, and all minded by a few dogs. The large fields were rich with corn, wheat, rye, tobacco, and indigo.

In the center of the land was a formidable two-story, white Dutch colonial mansion, made up of only the best in materials—no matter the distance nor the expense to buy—from its gambrel roof down to the fine glass windows under the lower-level overhangs. It was not only the home of his family, but also the servants, the cats, and on a daily basis Banshee, the rooster, attempted to get in. This was the Van Brunt domain that had entertained Sleepy Hollow guests for decades. Brom had only modernized it and made it outwardly more ostentatious.

Old Man Van Tassel had reigned over this land for some three decades, but the torch was passed to Brom on the day of his wedding to the old man's most treasured prize—his daughter. Over the last decade, Brom made every effort to make his own mark on the land. The Old Man still lived at the residence, and that was fine by Brom, because all the Old Man did was hobble around and smoke his favorite pipe—at that particular moment—in the nearest empty chair his bottom could find, inside or outside.

A horse-drawn wagon came through the gates. One of the townspeople was at the reins, but that was not what held Brom's attention. It was the men in the back of the wagon. They were doing their best to pretend that they had not seen him, as their sorry forms tried to slither down into the wagon out-of-sight.

The men were his. They all grew up together as children and were thick as thieves in their youth, accompanying him to anywhere there was a fight or trouble to be had. Brom and his Sleepy Hollow Boys. But they were grown men now, and he was their employer.

"What happened?" Brom's face was angry, and his hands grasped his waist.

"Well, Brom—"

"Mr. Van Brunt!" Brom corrected.

"Well, Mr. Van Brunt...he got the drop on us and..." Ace clutched his hat in his hand. "He got our horses."

"He took your horses from you? All three of you?" Brom shook his head. "If we didn't have history as friends, I'd run off all of you. But no one else would hire you good-for-nothings. Where is he?"

"We don't know, Mr. Van Brunt."

"Mr. Van Brunt, we can round up some of the men and go after him," Ayden suggested.

"So he can get those horses, too?" Brom waved them away. "Get to the field work."

"Yes, Mr. Van Brunt!" The men ran off to the barn.

The rider of the wagon was a local townsman who nervously smiled as he waited.

"This is some kind of business with this stranger in town," he said.

"Why are you still here?" Brom asked the man. "Are you waiting for something?"

"Mr. Van Brunt, I was thinking that since I had to go out of my way to return your men...that I'd get some kind of compensation for my trouble."

Brom's face went red. "The curse of the wealthy. Everyone is always anglin' to get into my pocket." He reached into his breast pocket and then threw a coin at the man. "Get out of here!"

The man let the coin fall into his lap and snapped the reins of the horses. The wagon did a complete circle to race back out the way it came.

Brom fumed as he walked back to the house as a cowboy in a fancy coat and large hat ambled toward him with a toothy smile.

"Yes, Mr. Van Brunt? No, Mr. Van Brunt. I can do that, Mr. Van Brunt," Dutch joked.

Brom was still angry. "The fools got their horses stolen from them by one man and were left on the side of the road. I don't like to me made a fool of. When my men are made to look foolish, I look foolish."

"What do you want done?"

"Find this man asking these questions."

"Who do you think he is?"

"That's what you'll find out, but I can tell you this much. This so-called inheritance man's story is a lie. No estate would wait ten years to conclude their business. He's here for some other no-good reason."

"No one can say what his name is."

"My point exactly. He's here for no-good. Five different people have already been here this morning to tell me about this compensation he's supposedly offering. Why would a stranger come here to the Hollow and stir up all these old feelings and memories? Scare the people? Give children nightmares? We've finally shaken free of the Legend, but this stranger will have people gossiping that the Horseman is back or is coming back. We're bringing in new people and with it new business, making the entire Tappan Zee area prosperous. Find him, find out what he's about, the true story, and move him along. Anywhere, but here."

"The horses?"

"Forget the horses. They want them back then let them go themselves to get them back. Let them walk until the soles of their shoes wear out, and they have to walk barefoot after that. That will teach them. All I'm interested in is finding this man."

"And when I do? What if he doesn't want to be moved along?"

Brom looked at him. "I've never had to spell it out before. What's different now?"

"This is no good, Brom. This stranger coming around asking questions after all this time."

"You don't think I know that? I want him gone. Out of the Hollow, out of Tarry Town, out of the entire region before Mrs. Van Brunt hears the first gossip about him. Gone. And I don't care how it's done. I never want to hear about him a fifth or sixth time, and I don't want to see him a first time. And I don't want to see you or your men until it's done. Understood?"

"We're riding out now."

Vengeance

"It is my extreme pleasure to meet you, Mr. Brom Bones. My name is Vengeance."

Katrina Van Brunt appeared at the top of the stairs in a fine blue dress, her golden blonde hair side-braided and resting on her shoulders. All the dresses she wore were only the best and most modern fashions, which took their cues from French and English trends. With her hand on the railing, she started down to see her attentive head maidservant waiting for her.

The mansion was quite large and flowed with the busy energy of the work activities of the servants, both male and female, indoors and outside, from sun-up to sundown.

"Mrs. De Paul, where is Mr. Van Brunt?" Katrina asked.

"Mr. Van Brunt is outside, ma'am. Should I send one of the houseboys to fetch him?"

"That won't be necessary. I see him at the gate."

Katrina gazed past her maidservant out the large front windows of the residence. She exited the mansion and stood on the porch watching her husband conduct his business with Dutch. She had become astute at divining whether the business was "legitimate" or "other."

She was the matriarch of the Van Brunt mansion, and the only child of Old Baltus Van Tassel, and many commented that she seemed to grow more radiant with time. She was only eighteen when she married Brom a decade ago. Folks told Brom that he was the fortunate one, but she always felt that it was an equal arrangement. She made him a better man, but every so often, he was tempted to revert back to his misbehaving ways he was infamous for in his youth. He noticed her watching, said a final word, and now made his way to the porch. Dutch headed to the main barn.

"Abraham, what is Dutch off to? I was going to have him hitch up the carriage to take me into town." She was the only person who called Brom by his true first name. The only person he allowed to.

"Why do you have to go into town again?"

"I need a few more things for the party."

Brom shook his head and sighed. "Ayden!" His call brought the man running. "Get the carriage and take Mrs. Van Brunt into town."

"Yes, Mr. Van Brunt."

Brom looked at her. "Please remember to leave something behind in the stores for the rest of the woman population."

She smiled as she walked over to him and planted a kiss on his cheek. "You do know that you're a grown man now with a position and reputation to maintain?"

He looked at her, not knowing what she meant.

She continued. "I married a man, not a boy. Men do adult things and attend to adult work. Sleepy Hollow Boys act about like children with mischief and trickery."

He knew what she meant now. "Dutch will be doing simple business in town for me."

She gave him a questioning look as Ayden came around front of the mansion driving the two-horse carriage. Brom walked to the carriage and opened the door for her. She allowed her husband to hold her steady with his hand as she climbed in, and then he closed the carriage door.

"Always remember, Abraham, I shall find out in the end," she said.

"Just remember what I said. Don't buy everything in the shops. We do live in this town with other people who like to buy things too."

Brom stepped back and nodded to Ayden. The carriage rode off to the main road to Tarry Town. He watched it silently until it was a ways away, over the hills, and gone.

Out of the barn came Dutch on his silver gray horse with seven other riders.

"Are you sure you don't want us to bring their horses back?"

"No. Let them do it. Teach 'em to not let a single man do that to them again."

Dutch nodded and motioned to his men to head out.

"Dutch!"

The men stopped.

"Mrs. Van Brunt is on her way into town too. See that she doesn't see you."

He smirked. "Understood, Mr. Van Brunt."

Brom's top man led the riders out, riding hard down the same main dirt road to Tarry Town.

The two-mile ride from Sleepy Hollow to Tarry Town was a quick ride for Dutch and his men. Every year seemed to bring more people looking for a decent place to settle and more visitors passing through. The Legend and every other haunted story were actually good for business in these parts, and there was no reason that the Hollow should get all the bounty.

"You've seen him then?"

Dutch asked one of the local townsmen outside the tavern. His four men stood around him, one smoking a cigar. He had sent the other three men to keep an eye on Mrs. Van Brunt's location so as to let him know if she came their way.

"The town has seen him, and everybody is talking about him. He's offering good money to find out the whereabouts of the last fool that the Horseman took," the man answered.

"That would be Hell, so he's wasting his time and everybody else's."

"He don't know that. He thinks that Ichabod the schoolteacher is still alive. You can tell. And he doesn't believe in the Legend." The man smiled wide. "Some of us are figuring we can trick him into giving us some of his reward money. One of us can pretend to be the unfortunate Ichabod and see if—"

"That's the most foolish thing I've heard," Dutch responded. "How do you figure that will work?"

"How would he know? He's never seen Ichabod before."

"Have you?"

"No, but we've heard him described enough times before. Skinny as a skeleton and funny big ears. What else is there to know?"

"You're a fool. But do whatever you like because we don't believe his real intention is to find Ichabod."

"Then why is he here?"

"That's why we're here!" Dutch was so frustrated with the man. He would have walked away but Jakes was one Tarry Town's chief busybodies who knew things before most and in these parts news traveled fast.

"Where did you see him last?" Dutch asked.

"I've seen him everywhere inquiring about Ichabod." The man's eyes looked up, thinking. "I think he was last at the church talking to the pastor."

"When was that?"

"Maybe an hour ago. He probably is still there. No, wait."

"What?"

"I don't see his horse. Everyone knows that horse of his now."

Dutch and his men turned to see where the man was looking.

"You didn't see him ride out?"

"No, I didn't. Me and the others have been keeping eyes on him. He must have double-backed somewhere."

Dutch looked around and said to a couple of his men, "You two go looking around for him."

As the two men quickly walked away, Dutch looked around at all the windows of the nearby shops and glanced down to the main inn.

"Maybe he's watching us right now," Dutch said softly. "I hear he's good at that."

The man looked around nervously.

"What is that you think this man is, if not what he

claims to be?"

"I think he's not what he claims to be. That's all I know, and I'd like to know a lot more before I leave town."

"Is there any money in it if I help you?"

"No, there isn't," Dutch said flatly. "But Mr. Van Brunt would be *grateful* for any help you could provide."

"Is he having a party tonight?"

Dutch looked at the man, already knowing what he was going to say.

"Can I come?"

Dutch sighed. "Yes, but—"

The man smiled again. "Let's go find him."

"Wait!" Dutch motioned to the man and his two remaining men. "Get out of sight."

The man didn't know why he was running, but he followed Dutch and his men into one of the shops. Once inside, they moved to the windows to watch the streets. The horse-drawn carriage of Mrs. Van Brunt galloped by.

"Why are you running away from your boss's wife?" the man asked, confused.

"Don't you worry about that," Dutch answered.

They all walked back outside.

Julian watched them quietly from across the street two shops down. He was already well hidden by the shade, but kept most of his body out of sight as he peered around the corner of the alleyway.

Katrina Van Brunt returned hours before, had a bath, and changed into her dress for the evening. The servants were busy at work in every corner of the mansion. The walls were adorned with lustrous items of silver, ears of Indian corn, ornate strings of red and green peppers, and dried fruits such as peaches and apples. The ceiling had strings of colored bird eggs suspended from it, and the mantelpiece was decorated with large conch shells and other smaller seashells. Expensive china adorned nearly every table or desktop, awaiting the servants to set dishes of food, drink and sweets.

Mr. Van Brunt had the field staff preparing for the arrival of the party guests. He strolled down the stairs in his finest evening clothes, purple to match his wife's dress, tugging on each sleeve.

"Where's your father?" he asked as soon as his wife crossed his path, moving quickly with candelabras in her hands. "Let the servants do that."

"He's sitting on the porch," she answered, ignoring his last statement and continuing on to the dining room.

Brom walked out on the porch and saw the man with his favorite evening pipe. He sat right next to him as Old Van Tassel exhaled a puff of smoke.

"It's going to be a fine party tonight, son."

"Yes sir, it will. They seem to get bigger every time we have one."

"Tarry Town will soon have to be called Tarry City with all the new people and families. Fifty years ago it was nothing but me and the Indians."

Brom had heard the story of the first days of Tarry Town and the Hollow from his father-in-law more times than he could count. The stories tended to go all night, especially when he was sitting comfortable with his pipe in mouth and his favorite cup of ale at his side.

The front door opened and Katrina popped out. "Abraham, and you, too, father, come on in and help us get ready. The first guests will be here any minute."

"I thought I was the man of the house," Brom said as he reluctantly stood up.

"I thought I was old," Mr. Van Tassel said as he reluctantly followed.

Even the field hands were in their best dress as the carriages began to arrive. Two men were at the main gate, and there was a whole system in place to direct the carriage drivers, open doors for passengers, and lead guests to the main house.

Three carriages arrived together. The couples exited and immediately greeted one another.

"Have you heard about this stranger inquiring about the Horseman's last victim?" one of the women asked.

"What was his name?" a man asked.

"Ichabod Crane. He was the schoolmaster. They closed it down when he disappeared," another man answered.

"Who is this stranger?" another man asked.

"Wasn't that seven years ago?" the man asked.

"He says he's working for some estate in New York City, or it might be Connecticut, to find Ichabod Crane so as to settle an estate. There's supposed to be some kind of compensation involved."

"More like ten years ago," a woman corrected.

"How much?"

"I haven't heard what the total amount is, but it's supposedly paid out whether they find him to be dead or alive."

"How about whisked away to hell? Do they have a third category for that?"

"People need to be careful about bringing up any of the

Horseman's victims," another woman warned. "Next, the Horseman himself will return and poor people will start to disappear all over again."

The warning ended the conversation as they walked to the front door.

Arriving guests were greeted by manservants, coats and hats were taken, and they were directed inside to be attended to by more servants. Brom stood inside with his wife on one side and Old Man Van Tassel on the other. The trio greeted arrivals in unison. The Old Man was still considered the chief patriarch of the Hollow. His daughter, Mrs. Van Brunt, was known far and wide for her charm, grace, and charity. Mr. Van Brunt was popular for another reason, besides the family wealth. He brought along family and friends alike as he moved up the social ladder and he was at the center of the region's new commercial growth. The children of the humble Dutch explorers that settled Sleepy Hollow long ago were now among the "who's who" of business in the state of New York—statehood had only been granted twelve years ago.

Brom chatted up the men, and Katrina gossiped with the women. People remarked on the finely carved furniture, but especially the food! The best culinary displays of Dutch New England food were everywhere—duck and turkey, sausages and sauces, bacon and hams, pies and cakes. Old Van Tassel made sure everyone had a hearty glass of wine or brandy, his ritual before he took a seat to smoke at one end of the piazza and gossip through the night of past times and old war stories.

Brom knew that any secrets of the stranger in town would soon dissipate. The chief female rumormongers of the town, a half dozen of them, had already cornered

Katrina. He had his own contingent to deal with.

"Surely, Mr. Van Brunt, you have heard about this stranger," said one of two men with him, talking and sipping his drink.

The loud laughter of Old Man Van Tassel frequently dinned above the conversations of the crowd, over sixty couples, and even the music of the pianist, a German-born man from outside of Sing Sing. The men were in their best and most expensive coats and breeches, white stockings, and buckled shoes, while the women were in their most expensive hooped dresses or frocks.

"I heard," Brom answered the man. "It's a free country. He'll come and he'll go. I have more important things to concern myself with."

Something told Brom to glance at his wife. She shot him a look as she continued talking with the women, pretending to be hanging on their every word.

"Does anyone know where he's from?" Brom asked.

"Someone said upstate New York, or maybe it was Connecticut?"

"Meaning, no one knows."

The front door opened and a manservant greeted him.

"Your hat and coat, sir?"

Julian handed them to him.

"Who may I say is here, sir?"

"No need, sir. I'm a surprise for the man of the house. Just show me the way to good ol' Brom."

The butler smiled. Only a true friend of Mr. Van Brunt would call him Brom.

"Yes, of course, sir."

Brom and Katrina had joined each other again with

many other couples listening to the latest and hilarious stories from Mr. Peters. The man had become the center of the party, and Old Man Van Tassel, the usual honoree of that position, was as eager to hear as anyone else. What gathering at a home in the Hollow would be complete without a good ol' nighttime ghost story?

"It was the Ghost of Raven Rock. A temptress that haunts that dark glen and can be heard shrieking on winter nights before a storm." Mr. Peters lifted both hands up, contorted his hands to make them seem like claws, and widened his eyes in fake horror. Everyone else drew near with smiles and laughter.

Brom barely noticed the man walk into the room, and he wouldn't have noticed him at all, if not for the cold stare. He had never seen the man before, but there he stood looking directly at him.

"Who is that man?" Katrina asked. She had already noticed the man, too.

"I don't know. I shall find out."

Brom excused himself and set his drink on the corner table, which was promptly picked up by one of the servants. As Brom approached the man, he had an instant thought of as to who the stranger might be.

"Good evening, sir," Brom said. "I don't believe I've had the pleasure of meeting you. Who might you be?"

"No, but our accounts have preceded us both." The young man's tone had a tangible anger to it.

"I don't like to have my simple questions answered by riddles. Who are you?" Brom decided to match his rude tone.

The man continued. "Abraham Van Brunt. Known more commonly as Brom Bones—"

"Who are you? And why are you in my house? You are not an invited guest."

Brom's outburst brought every conversation in the mansion to an abrupt halt. This was another thing that he was known for—his volcanic temper whenever it was provoked. He was the embodiment of a bull ready to charge its prey as his face reddened and fists clenched.

The man yelled back, "My name is Julian Crane! And I'm here to hunt down the foul murderer of my uncle, the late Mr. Ichabod Crane! That foul murderer is you!" Julian pointed a finger at him. "You, Brom Bones! The death blood of my uncle is on your hands! You, Brom Bones!"

Trouble

"Run this Julian Crane out of the Hollow! And do it in a way that he shall never, ever return!"

No one had ever seen such an expression on Brom Bones. The color had left his face and he transformed from a projectile ready to launch to that of a proverbial, derailed wagon capable of no further movement.

The partygoers all stood there with mouths hanging open, speechless and shocked. The color had even left the rosy cheeks of Katrina Van Brunt, who also stood frozen.

Brom glanced at crowd, turned and marched out of the mansion's front door.

Everyone looked at one another. Now all eyes were focused on the man.

Katrina's voice started softly at first, but grew in intensity. "Mr. Julian Crane, if that is truly your name." She approached him as she spoke. "You are to leave my house this instant without delay, or I shall have you snatched by the throat and thrown off my property."

Julian paused a moment. A manservant walked up to him as if on cue and handed him his hat and coat. Julian turned to Mrs. Van Brunt and said, "You shall be seeing me again."

"Oh yes, Mr. Julian Crane, I have no doubt of that. But, I suspect, it will be at a time and a place and in a manner far from your liking."

Julian had only walked a few steps when he turned back to her. "I believe this is how it transpired for my poor uncle. He left this very house, probably at this very hour, only to have the misfortune of coming upon your husband on a deserted road in the night masquerading as this imaginary Headless Horseman. Tell your husband, Mrs. Van Brunt, that should I come across any ghost or goblin on my way, I shall greet it with a blast from my rifle, and I never miss."

Katrina looked at him with contempt, but it was just a mask over other emotions. Where was Brom?

"My husband did no such thing ever!" she yelled.

"Sir, please leave now," the manservant said to Julian, as he motioned him to the door. "We do not want to resort to forcibly escorting you off the Van Brunt land."

Pandemonium! Guests vacated the mansion as fast as their feet could move. Field hands got their drivers. Drivers rode their horse-drawn carriages and wagons from the spacious Van Brunt stables and barns to the front of the mansion, and then, with their passengers aboard, raced out to all points in the Hollow and beyond, with drivers holding lanterns to illuminate the darkness.

Dutch and his men returned. They rode up to the main gate as one of the guest carriages flew past. Dutch dismounted and quickly walked to Ace, who was in a frantic state talking with a couple of house servants, one holding a lantern.

"What happened?" Dutch asked.

"Where were you?" Ace yelled at him. "He was here!"

"Who? The stranger?"

"Yes! He's Ichabod Crane's nephew! He waltzed right into the middle of the mansion and accused Brom of killing him, right in front of a hundred people!"

"Killing who?"

"Ichabod Crane! He accused Brom of killing Ichabod Crane!"

"What did you do?"

"Me? I was out here. We only learned of him when everyone started rushing out for their carriages." Ace shook his head in distress. "People are going to spread these lies all across the entire eastern seaboard."

"I got to see Brom now," Dutch said.

Ace jumped in front of him. "He's not seeing anyone. Not a living soul. Mrs. Van Brunt shouted at everyone to leave, and she even told all of the house servants to get out."

Dutch stopped and scratched his chin.

Ace pointed at him. "You were supposed to take care of him and now look what's happened. He may have stolen our horses, but you let him ruin Brom's name. He'll never forgive you for this."

Dutch gave him a look of casual disregard and jumped back on his horse. "We'll find him. How far can he get on a night like this? A stranger, unfamiliar with our roads. He won't get far at all."

None of them saw it coming. The projectile flew out of the night and hit the man in his face. Dutch screamed out as he fell off his horse.

His seven riders galloped in and surrounded him with guns drawn, frightened. Ace grabbed the lantern from the two servants. Both servants didn't wait and quickly ran away. Ace had barely pulled his own pistol when another orange projectile landed near the lead horseman, startling all of the men again. They looked out into the night, ready to shoot, but saw no one.

"I know this is how you did my uncle!" a voice yelled out from the darkness. "But I'm watching all of you! If you step anywhere near me, no one is going to say you were 'taken' by the Horseman! They're going to say you were shot stone dead by my rifle! Last time I took your horses! Next time our paths cross, it will be your life!"

Julian's voice was gone.

Dutch stood from the ground, his face wet and covered with fragments of the shattered pumpkin lying at his feet.

They could barely make out hoof sounds in the distance. The full moon was bright in the sky.

Julian rested on the bed, staring up at the ceiling. His coat was thrown on the chair near a small desk, and his hat hung on the back of the chair. His boots were still on, the heels hanging slightly over the edge of the single bed. The desk had his satchel and a few more fist-sized pumpkins — his newfound projectile of choice. He hadn't slept a wink last night, and doubted he'd be sleeping now or any time tonight, no matter how tired he might be. But he wasn't tired.

It was a simple single-occupancy room for rent on the second floor of the inn. He could hear voices in the room next to his, beyond the wall nearest his head on the pillow. The window was open and he could hear the comings and goings of people, horses, wagons, the whole lot, outside for a new morning day.

Knock! Knock!

Julian's eyes slowing turned to the door. His hand tightened around his rifle right next to him in the bed.

Knock! Knock!

Julian didn't open the door slowly, he threw it open violently. The man in the hallway was startled as he nervously stood there. It was innkeeper. He held out his arms to his side, his hands clearly visible, and his hat tilted back so his face was fully visible. There were no weapons on his person.

"I'm just the messenger, mister," he said. "I don't want any trouble in my place of business." He waited.

Julian stood there with most of his body off to the side of the door entrance. The man couldn't see it, but he knew Julian was holding a weapon. It was probably the same rifle that Julian went to great care to make sure everyone saw when he checked in this morning.

"Mister, some of the town elders would like to speak with you."

"Why?"

"They'll speak directly to you about their business."

Julian backed away from the open door slowly to keep his eye on the man. With his rifle clutched firmly in his hand, he turned briefly and grabbed his hat.

"It's not personal, but if you're leading me into a trap, I'll shoot you first, no matter what. That would be the only fair thing to do."

"Yes, it would. But again mister, I'm only a messenger."

"I'll follow."

The man led Julian downstairs to the lobby desk where several distinguished-looking men waited in fancy suits, shiny shoes, and top hats.

"Mr. Julian Crane?" one of them asked.

"Yes?"

"We apologize for the interruption, but as the elected elders of Tarry Town, we had to speak with you."

"Brom Bones has many friends in high places." Julian made the comment more to himself.

"Mister, this has nothing to do with Mr. Van Brunt. This concerns the safety and well-being of the town. We are sorry, but we must ask you to leave the town."

"Why?" Julian asked abruptly. "I am an ex-soldier of the Continental Army, a citizen of this state of New York, and I go and stay anywhere in these United States that I please. I thought this town was on the right side in the War."

The men were visibly ruffled by his insinuation.

"Mister, we were all on the *right* side in the War," the man in the largest stove top hat said in a gruff voice. "We also have the wounds and gravesites to prove it. Our request is not meant as any show of disrespect, but as the official leaders of the town, we have an obligation to keep any trouble from it. News flies fast in these parts. You have put yourself on the opposite side of the most powerful man in the region, for what reason we do not care, but he will have more than just words with you when he finds you. We can't have any gunplay in the town. This is a booming town, but it is also a quiet and respectable one with decent families, and decent folk. Surely, you can understand our position."

"Please be reasonable, mister. Your quarrel is in Sleepy

Hollow, but you're bringing it to Tarry Town," another man added.

"That's why I came here," Julian said. "Brom Bones owns Sleepy Hollow."

"Mr. Van Brunt owns Tarry Town, too, mister," a third man interjected. "That's why you need to leave this whole region."

"So the murderer is a hero of these parts, is he?" Julian asked bitterly.

"Murderer? Who did Mr. Van Brunt murder?" the largest man asked.

"What false accusations are you bringing against him?" another man added defiantly.

"The late Ichabod Crane!" Julian yelled at men.

The Elders glanced at one another.

"Do you have proof of what you say, mister?" the largest man asked.

"Why do you think I am here?" Julian snapped.

"Then why haven't you brought that proof to the law?"

"Why? So a jury of his peers—his employees, friends and neighbors—could set him free? No. I'll handle this in my way, which will still be better than the way he killed my uncle, stalking him in the middle of the night as if my uncle were some defenseless animal. Probably shot my poor uncle in the back."

"Mister, I've known Brom from the time he was a toddler, and he never shot any man in the back. If he comes for you, he'll come at you straight. You'll see him coming full on."

"Really? And he never dressed up as this imaginary Headless Horsemen and came at people in the dark of night? Because that's not what I heard."

The men's expression changed to nervousness.

"Mister, I don't know who's been filling your head with tales, but even if that were true, harmless pranks are something altogether different. Every young boy has done those in his life. I have, as have all my colleagues here, and I bet you have."

"None of my pranks ever killed anybody."

The largest of the men in the stove top hat watched Julian for a moment and then said, "You know what concerns me about you, mister? It would appear that the reason for you taking the law in your own hands is that you don't have any proof whatsoever to take before a magistrate or jury. You have plenty of wild speculation, but no proof. If you ever yelled out such a thing in a crowded place, a gross accusation to tarnish a man's good name with no proof, you would be deserving of the mess of trouble you would receive. Go home, young man. Brom didn't kill anybody, and he didn't kill Ichabod Crane."

"Brom killed Ichabod because he wanted him out of the way to marry Katrina Van Tassel. He dressed up as this imaginary Headless Horseman, chased him down in the night, and killed him. Where he disposed of the body is the only thing I don't know. That's what happened, and I shall not allow him to get away with the crime. My poor uncle deserved a better death in life than to be run down in the middle of night like a rabid dog."

"Mister, we're sorry, but you must leave this town. The first lawman who gets back into town will arrest you, not him, for plotting murder. And if the law doesn't arrive in time, Brom never killed anyone, but he will kill you, or his men will, out of justified self-defense."

"How did Brom kill Ichabod?" another man asked with

a disgusted look on his face.

"What?" Julian asked.

"You heard me. How did he kill him? You are so certain of it. How did he do it?"

"I know he killed him. Someone saw him do it!"

None of the men were impressed. None of them believed him.

"Who would that be?" the man asked.

"Why? So you can tell Brom Bones, and this imaginary Headless Horseman can suddenly appear to take the witness away in the night, too? I'll keep the information to myself."

"Young man, if you have a true witness, then you are obligated to take him to the law."

"I shall do it my way."

"Young man, we have already sent for the U.S. Marshal. We are not going to allow gunplay in our streets with families and children."

"There will be no great gun battle, only my bullet shot into the carcass of one Brom Bones."

"We cannot allow that, mister."

The largest man lunged at Julian. The other men jumped forward, too. Julian smacked the first man's face so hard that he stumbled back into the other men.

"The Elders of Tarry Town reveal their true loyalties!" Julian's face was flush with anger as he aimed his rifle at them.

"Mister, we would do the same if it were Brom. You two will not be allowed to accidentally kill any of our men, women, or children in this town. That's what always happens when two men set on killing arrive in the same town."

"Mr. Julian Crane, get your things and the inn will refund your money," the innkeeper added. "We have the right to refuse our welcome to anyone and ask them to leave."

"I thought you reserved that right for Indians and Negroes."

The men gave him an odd look.

"Mister, we are fast growing from simple farming towns to great trading centers of the Mid-Atlantic states," the large man said. "But every man standing here is also a member of the New York Manumission Society, despite the sentiments of other parts of the state. Many of us were members of abolition societies before people even knew what abolition meant. The Negroes formerly of this area are in New York City hoping to create the first free-black township in the state. I was there a few months ago. Do you wish to join my wife and I when we visit again?"

"We told the last pro-slavery folks that passed through here to keep on passing through far away from here," the man next to him said.

"Mister, you have an unpleasant way about you," another man said. "These parts have also always been good to the Indians. We fought side-by-side against the Red Coats. The Indians and Whites who fought with the British, we equally have no use for."

"I don't care if you fought on the same as us in the War," the large man said. "You are a real bastard, Mr. Julian Crane, and we are starting to dislike you immensely."

Julian moved back, still aiming his rifle. "Then I must get back in your good graces. You don't have to send for the U.S. Marshal."

"Why is that?"

"I sent for him two weeks ago before my arrival. I anticipated this friendly reception from the townspeople. He'll be here soon, and I expect to have Brom's dead body waiting for him. That's why I'm here. Not to cause trouble, but to wait for the marshal. But I know that murderer Brom Bones will seek me out, so it will be a righteous shooting of self-defense. Me, defending myself against him."

Julian's head leaned forward and he pointed at one of the men. "You're bleeding."

"What?" the elder asked.

"Oh, for goodness sake," De Graaf chimed in. "Your nose is bleeding."

The man touched his nose and drops of blood dripped down and dotted the wooden floor. He quickly snatched his handkerchief from his pocket and covered his nose."

Julian lowered his rifle and walked back up the stairs. He kept his eyes on them until he disappeared from sight. "Don't come to my room again," his voice yelled out.

"Mr. Julian Crane, we're surely not going to take your word that you called the marshal yourself, so we'll be doing that immediately!" an elder yelled after him, though they knew he was already back in his room.

De Graaf looked at the man with the bleeding nose. "He didn't do that did he? I didn't see him hit you."

"He didn't do anything. It just starts bleeding whenever the weather's going to be bad or there's going to be trouble."

Dutch and his posse trotted slowly to town. There was no need to rush, as they already knew where he was. On his right was his best man, and on his left were two of the next best. He was especially keen to settle the score with this stranger for what he did to his boss, Ace and the others. Four more men followed behind them.

"This time we get him," Dutch called out. "There's no back doors or trees or darkness for him to hide in this time. We get him, and we don't leave until we do."

Julian walked down second floor hallway past his room to the door at the end. He firmly knocked once. There was movement inside and then the door opened slowly. A chubby man appeared.

"It's time," Julian said. "Go out now and get your wagon."

"All you want us to do is drive?" the man asked as another hand opened the door wider. Two other men stood there. All of them were sleeping.

"That's what I'm paying you for. And where did you hide my horse?"

"He's mixed in with Mr. Flander's in his barn on the other side of town."

"Good, go now. It should be happening soon."

"I hope you know what you're doing, mister."

"Why do you care? You don't live here and you're getting paid. Go now so that no one sees you."

The Elders stood outside the front of the inn talking so loudly and frantically that people in the town were starting to gather in the street. Dutch and his men rode up on their horses.

"He says he has a witness to Ichabod's murder! You didn't tell us—" the main elder started to say.

"He's lying!" Dutch yelled. "Brom didn't kill nobody! The Horseman took him. We all know that. What room is he in?"

"Dutch, we can't have gunplay here," the innkeeper said.

"There won't be. Give me the master key to the room and we'll get him. There's eight of us and just one of him."

The Elders looked to De Graaf. The large man nodded reluctantly to one of the men. The proprietor of the inn walked back inside and returned in an instant with a large key in his hand. Dutch leaned down from his horse and grabbed it.

"Dutch," the main elder said. "No gunplay. No killing. Just take him and go."

Dutch smiled. "Of course, Mr. De Graaf. Mr. Van Brunt is an elder of the town, too, and wants to maintain the peace as much as you do."

Dutch got down from his horse and his men did the same. He looked at them as they all drew their guns. They left the horses where they stood and walked into the inn.

Warpath

"I want Julian Crane dead!"

The three men couldn't hide the nervous shock on their faces. None of them were accustomed to seeing so much blood. They madly rode the wagon as fast as their two horses could go. One the men tried with all his might not to look, but he couldn't control himself. He turned his head to look again at the original sight that so distressed them. In the wagon was a pile of bloody bodies with a battered Julian sitting Indian-style in the center of them, looking back at him.

The men shuddered to think what a savage beating he must have given them.

The dining table took up almost the entire length of the room, and the room was by no means small. It was perfect for hosting their home parties, though they did not use it last night. It was more often used for meetings rather than family meals, as it was too ostentatious for Brom, even in his role as a wealthy businessman of the region. He sat at the head of the table, gently holding his wife's soft hand.

He peered at her from his corner chair as if he were on trial. But then he was.

"It wasn't me," Brom pleaded. "It is all lies."

"Why is this stranger so convinced then?" she retorted.

"He's a stranger. Who knows what is in his mind. I doubt he is even his nephew. Ichabod had no family and no relatives."

"That we know of," Katrina corrected.

"Look into my eyes and you tell me if I would do such a horrible thing, could do what he is accusing. It's all lies."

For a long time they stared at each other without a word said.

"I would never do such a horrible thing," he repeated. "Playing pranks on a man is one thing, but murder? This stranger is lying, and I will get to the bottom of it."

"Abraham, let the law handle it. We can stay away from him until the marshal arrives."

Brom jumped up from the table. "So he can continue spreading his lies? So he can continue to ruin my good name and yours? No, I cannot allow this to continue."

They could both hear voices outside, but ignored them.

She sighed. "It has already happened, and there's not a thing we can do to stop it at this point. When the marshal arrives, you can defend yourself publicly and properly. Abraham, Sleepy Hollow isn't a tiny town anymore. It will one day soon be a sizable city that will continue to grow. We have to do things proper. We can't have men settling their quarrels with duels and shoot-outs. Do it that way and people will doubt you. Besides, he hasn't provided one bit of proof to anyone."

Brom returned to his chair. "Precisely. That's why I'm so angry. Everyone believes a lie instantly, but the truth takes a whole week to digest. I should know."

Katrina grins. "Yes, you and your gang did it to plenty of people before."

Brom nods. "That's the past. I gave that all up when I married you."

The voices and commotion outside the room had now grown louder, attracting their full attention. The Van Brunts got up from their chairs and walked out of the dining room. The agitated voices came from outside the house. Mrs. De Paul, the head maidservant, came out of the kitchen to also see what the disturbance was.

The front door flew open and Jansen, the head manservant, rushed in.

"Mr. Van Brunt!" He immediately stopped as he saw them. "Come quick!"

"What's happening?" Brom asked.

Jansen led Brom outside, both men running.

The spot was a quarter mile away. At the main gate, all the field hands were gathered.

"What is this? Get back to work!" Brom yelled.

Jansen pointed at the tree and stopped. Major Andre's tree was an enormous tulip tree that towered over all other trees on the land. It was said to be older than the Hollow itself, far older than fifty years. Its limbs were massive and twisted down to the ground and rose back into the air. At night, the sight of the tree with its gnarled limbs gave rise to many a ghost story.

Major Andre was a real person. He was a Tarry Town man who had the misfortune of being taken prisoner by the British during the War. The tree bore his name out of respect, and out of superstition as it, too, at least in many years past, was said to be haunted by the unlucky man.

Nowadays, it was considered a natural landmark of the Hollow.

Brom neared the tree, but he could not believe what he was seeing. Jansen and other field hands followed closely behind. He saw his men, his enforcers—bound, gagged and strung up, hanging upside down from the tree by their feet—Dutch and all seven of his cowboys. From their bruises, cuts, and the dry blood on their faces, it must have been an epic battle. One they lost and paid the humiliating price.

"Cut them down!" Brom yelled. His face was so red with rage that he seemed like he'd explode.

Ayden recoiled when Brom turned to glare at him. He feared what Brom might do at that instant.

"I want every man armed with whatever gun or rifle that can be put in their hand and ready to ride within the hour." He looked at his head butler. "You, too, Jansen! And have all the male servants in the house do the same!"

Jansen knew better not to protest. He kept his mouth shut.

A red-haired man, one of the townsmen, frantically rode into Tarry Town. From the expression on his face, people casually conducting their business stopped what they were doing—walking, talking, etc.—and took notice of him. He jumped down from his horse and ran to the inn where the town elders waited.

"It's bad, Mr. De Graaf. Brom is unleashing a posse. He's going to hunt down and kill that man who says he's Ichabod Crane's nephew. There's no stopping it."

The Elders looked at one another with dismay.

"What happened to Dutch and his men?" De Graaf

asked.

"The stranger beat them nearly to death and strung them up from Major Andre's Tree."

"How on earth could one man do all that to eight men?" an elder asked.

"We don't know, but he did. And now Brom is a volcano of anger on his way here to settle the score."

"This is exactly what we were trying to prevent," another elder said.

"What do we do?" another asked.

"We have no choice but to swear in some temporary lawmen and take him into custody for his own safety and for the safety of the town," De Graaf decided.

"But we don't even know what happened exactly," an elder said. "I can't believe this supposed nephew of Ichabod Crane could do what he did to Brom's men. Dutch is a former lawman himself. He couldn't be done like that by one man."

"If Mr. Van Brunt is gathering a posse, then we know it was bad, and that's all we need to know at this time," De Graaf answered. "We must act quickly. Koning, get all the townspeople off the streets. Boer, take De Wit and station yourselves at the entrance into town. Maybe you can say something to Brom and at least get him to think or slow the posse down, even if it's for a short time. I'll be there, too. For now, I'll appoint as many temporary lawmen as we can find."

The streets were abnormally crowded as people congregated in groups, large and small, eager for any news they could get about what had the town in such a frenzy and the coming of Brom's posse for Ichabod's nephew.

"I knew the man was all about trouble," one of the townsmen said.

One of the groups contained an over-representation of people who had personally met or come across Julian Crane.

"Did you hear?" a woman asked.

"What did we hear?" a man responded.

"Brom's coming to town with every man he has to get this stranger claimin' to be Ichabod's relative."

"No?"

"Yes. The showdown is coming any minute now."

"A gun battle in Tarry Town?"

"What'd the stranger do?" a man asked.

"I heard he butchered Brom's men in cold blood…with an ax! And he's not poor Ichabod's nephew but actually an agent of the devil Horseman himself."

"No," the entire crowd exclaimed in shock.

"Yes," the man continued. "That's what I heard."

"I knew there was something about him. I knew it."

"You knew nothing. You wanted that inheritance reward money like everyone else."

The man blushed.

"Where's the law in all this? If he kilt Brom's men, where are they?"

"They sent for the marshal."

"Oh, no," Mrs. Van Boor said aloud.

"What?" her husband asked.

"We had the stranger in our own house…if he's an agent of the Horseman…could he—?"

"Stop that talk. Could he nothing!"

He hugged her to acknowledge that he did take her fears seriously.

"Mr. Van Brunt is going to put an end to this whole thing today. You'll see."

"What do we do if we see him?"

"What do you mean? Why do anything?"

"If he's an agent of the Horseman, shouldn't we do something?"

"Yes. Run the other way."

Some of the people in the gathering laughed

"No, I'm serious. He could mark us."

"Mark us? What does that mean?"

"Just like they say those witches do," the man continued.

"Mark us how?"

"If he touches us or comes into close proximity to us, he could mark us for the Horseman. Mark us for its return."

"Oh my God," Mrs. Van Boor called out.

"Stop frightening my wife!"

"Stop frightening all of us," another man said.

The panic was growing. They all had been in close proximity with the stranger.

"How many here had the stranger in their homes?"

No one answered, but everyone knew who those people were.

"How many here had contact with the stranger?"

"We should shoot him," a new man said.

The entire group of townspeople looked at him.

"We should shoot him on sight. He may be an agent of the Horseman, but he's still flesh and blood like us for the moment. Until he makes whatever final devil pact with the Horseman."

"I've never heard such nonsense," a deep voice called out.

De Graaf stood at the edge of the crowd.

"I have now seen with my own eyes how mass hysteria comes about. I leave this group alone long enough, and I'm more frightened of what schemes you'll come up with. When you're finished with your group rantings, you'll say he's the Horseman."

"Oh my God," an older man interjected. "Mr. De Graaf, that's it! He's the Horseman. It's taken human form to spy on us."

De Graaf couldn't believe his ears. "I was not being serious!"

"But Mr. De Graaf—"

"No, I forbid any of you to talk. You are making up your own tales of terror right here on the streets of Tarry Town. And I thought Sleepy Hollow folk were bad."

"Mr. De Graaf, we all live in Sleepy Hollow."

"There it is. But before you continue…This Julian Crane did not murder Mr. Van Brunt's men with an ax, any weapon or instrument, or his bare hands. He beat them bloody, yes, and strung them up, but they are all quite alive. That's what happened."

"But Mr. De Graaf, we heard—"

"That's exactly the problem. You're hearing the wrong things and then spreading your false gossip to create fear and panic. My duty is the safety of Tarry Town. In keeping with that, I am ordering you all off the streets. There could be some very dangerous gunplay today, and someone could get murdered for real. Everyone get off the streets now and go home. And no more gossiping about this unless you talk to me about it. Telling tales around the fireplace is the nightly ritual in these parts. Telling tales as facts outside is reckless and dangerous. We are adults not schoolchildren. Go home now, please. For your safety."

The people were reluctant but listened to him and began to clear the streets.

De Graaf noticed three couples standing back, waiting to leave last, waiting for him. Dressing in black was common, but their dark clothes seemed to have a more ominous look with their gaunt bodies and drawn faces.

"Maybe this J. Crane isn't the Horseman," one of the women said. "Maybe he didn't murder anyone that we know of. Perhaps he's not an agent of the Horseman. But I don't believe in coincidences, and I'm sure you don't either, Mr. De Graaf. The Horseman's been gone for more than ten years after it took Ichabod Crane. I don't believe for an instant that the resurrection of all this Legend talk and Ichabod talk isn't going to bring the Horseman galloping back to Sleepy Hollow so that its deathly search for victims can start again. Tell me that isn't the case. Look me right in the eye, Mr. De Graaf, and tell us here, now."

De Graaf said nothing back to her.

Mr. Berg, the undertaker, leaned against the wall of his mortuary with his pipe hanging from his lips. He watched people gather in the street and disperse over and over, and people coming and going all because of the anticipated showdown.

It could be a busy day indeed today.

"You shouldn't be so self-satisfied, Mr. Berg. It's unseemly," a townsman said to him.

Berg turned to see the man watching him with a look of disapproval.

"Why shouldn't I be happy in the anticipation of some business? I'm an undertaker, and I need bodies to take under." He laughed.

"I'm glad death is funny to you."

"Why shouldn't it be funny to everyone? You can cry about it. Be sad about it. Be scared about it. I choose to be happy about it. Not that any emotion makes the slightest bit of difference. Death is going to come. Only the when and how is an open question."

"If you say."

"Do you know when Brom and his men will arrive?"

"It won't be long. I heard he already left the Van Brunt place."

"Soon." Berg smiled.

"Think this stranger will get any of them before he goes down?"

"This stranger is a clever one. I'm not convinced he'll go down after all. If it's gotten to this point where Brom has to get a whole big gang of his men to come with such force in the open like this, it means this stranger has bested everything Brom has thrown at him. This is Brom's final play, but I don't think it's the last play for this stranger."

"You say what you want. Brom's gang rides into town, and this stranger is shot dead right at the start. Bam. Dead. Only one body for you."

"We shall see."

Julian Crane sat at the rear table alone, nursing his wounds. It was only a cut above his eye and a bruise to his right temple. Mild compared to what he inflicted on his eight attackers. He had a plate of untouched food in front of him. His main activity was soaking a cloth in a pitcher of water and applying slight pressure to his cut. He had already wiped the butt of his rifle clean of all the blood from his victims.

The tavern was not packed, but everyone present had their eyes on him. Some people were very quiet, while others whispered amongst themselves. "It's that man claiming to be Ichabod's nephew." "Ichabod Crane, the one taken by the Horseman."

"Are you really Ichabod Crane's nephew?" The tavern owner stood across from his table.

"I am."

"Ichabod had no kin, so how could he have a nephew?"

"Ichabod had an older, estranged brother. My father."

"Had?"

"Killed in the War."

"Oh." The tavern owner was sorry he had pried. "I lost a boy in the War." The owner paused for a moment. "Is it true? You accused Brom Bones of killing your uncle?"

"I did."

"Your uncle was killed by the Horseman, mister."

"There is no such thing! That's imaginary superstition!" Julian was angry.

"The Headless Horseman isn't imaginary!" The owner was angrier.

"This is the year 1800, and there is no such thing as ghosts and undead creatures. The earth is not flat, and there is no Headless Horseman. Murderers are all men. The only exception is the rare times when it's a woman."

"Stranger, you're going to meet a terrible end. It'll either be Brom, for spreading lies about him, or the Horseman, because your fool self will go looking for it. Either way, you're going to meet a terrible end."

"The only person who'll meet a terrible end is the murderer of my uncle, Brom Bones."

The owner had turned in a huff, but stopped in his tracks. Julian looked up to see about a dozen armed men approaching with the Elders following.

Julian grinned to himself. The men reached his table and De Graaf, the head elder, pushed through to the front.

"I notice in these parts the people like to gang up on a man," Julian said. "Three to one, eight to one, fifteen to one."

"Mr. Julian Crane, if that is your true name, we are taking you into custody," De Graaf announced.

"On what charges?"

"On the charge that you are a menace to this town and we are not going to allow any gunplay in our streets," the head elder answered. "Do you know that Mr. Van Brunt is heading to town with a full posse to find and probably kill you?"

"I suspected he might do such. I'm waiting for him," Julian answered.

"Please stand up, mister," the head deputy said to him.

"Not until you take the letter from my left breast pocket."

"Why?" the head deputy asked.

"Because it's addressed to you."

The deputies looked to De Graaf for instructions. He nodded to them. Julian slowly opened his coat, and the main deputy reached into the pocket. The letter inside was a cream color and had an official look to it.

The deputy carefully opened it and read to the end. He looked up and then read it again.

"What does it say?" De Graaf asked impatiently.

The deputy handed him the letter.

"I suspect, as a fellow abolitionist, you will be duly

impressed by my benefactor," Julian added in a quiet tone.

The men had no notion of what he meant. The Elders gathered around De Graaf as they all read it. De Graaf finished first and looked at Julian, shaking his head.

"My letter, please." Julian stood and reached out his hand.

De Graaf handed him back the letter. Julian returned it to his inside breast pocket and then threw a few coins on the table. "Thank you for the fine meal, sir," he said to the owner. He turned back to the deputies. "Get out of my way."

The deputies looked to De Graaf for direction. De Graaf said, "Let him go."

The deputies moved back and Julian walked past them. He stopped in front of De Graaf. "This is the last time I am going to allow you to get in my way. I am going to avenge the murder of my uncle, and if you ever get in my way again—" He didn't finish the sentence. "This is between Mr. Brom Bones and me. Not you, your elders, your town, or any imaginary horseman. Don't make me have this conversation with you again."

Julian walked out of the tavern without anyone stopping him.

"What just happened?" one of the new deputies asked. "You appointed us as lawmen and then you let him walk out free. What did the letter say?"

De Graaf recited it from memory. "To whom it may concern. Mr. Julian Crane has been duly appointed as a provisional U.S. Marshal of the State of New York to investigate the murder of his family member, one Ichabod Crane. All local authorities are to render any and all assistance. Signed, John Jay, Governor of the State of New York."

Showdown

"I want Brom Bones dead!"

John Jay was not only the Governor of New York. He was one of the Founding Fathers, one of the fifty-six signers of the Declaration of Independence, one of the three authors of the Federalist Papers, the first Chief Justice of the Supreme Court, and the state's leading abolitionist, signing into law just the year before an act for the gradual emancipation of all slaves in New York, in the face of the continued growth of the institution in the new state. With a letter of such significance, Julian Crane was untouchable to them, and he was right — this would be a battle between him and Brom Bones, and no other.

Brom's posse would arrive in town at any moment. Julian settled his bill with the owner of the barn where he was staying. The fidgety man was anxious to get him out and away as fast as humanly possible. Everyone knew what was coming.

Julian looked at the bloody rag he pulled from his pocket. Dutch was the only one of the men who managed to hit him with any kind of blow, but it was minor. But looking at the rag he used to wipe the wound, it looked like he had wiped up a gallon of blood from his face. He couldn't stop staring at it. This was an unnatural place.

He turned and there she was waiting—Katrina Van Brunt.

Julian continued out of the barn but did not move closer to her.

"Morning, Mrs. Van Brunt."

She was annoyed he didn't stop. "You have about fifteen minutes to get on your horse and ride out of here for dear life before they arrive."

"Yes, they told me about the Brom Bones posse. Did you want to see my face one last time? Or are you going snatch me by the throat, as you threatened at your home, and hold me down until your husband arrives to kill me? Though the sun is out and I know he likes to do his evil deeds at night."

"Mr. Crane, what evidence do you have my husband killed your uncle? Because all I have heard from you is overblown talk. What evidence do you have that Ichabod is even dead? There are rumors that he's living in—"

Julian interrupted her. "Yes, he's living in upstate New York. He runs his own private school. He became a lawyer. He became a politician. He became a judge of the court. He went back to Connecticut or went to Kentucky where he wanted to take you as his wife. Or the state of Tennessee."

Katrina swallowed hard. Julian did seem to have knowledge that could only have come directly from Ichabod.

Julian continued. "Mrs. Brunt, I rode through every major town in Northern New York, Connecticut,

Kentucky, and Tennessee before I rode here to Sleepy Hollow. I sent out queries to every lawman in every surrounding state, even though I didn't need to. My uncle Ichabod was fanatical about keeping his habits. In his eye, he probably knew no other states existed outside New York and Connecticut, and he fixated on Kentucky and Tennessee only because he met a fellow singing master from there and became enchanted with the accounts of the states. No, Mrs. Van Brunt, my uncle Ichabod is dead. I have no doubt of it in my soul."

"Mr. Crane, you have an idealized view of your uncle. He was a good man, a gentleman and a learned man, whose knowledge was only inferior to our late parson. But let's be clear. Ichabod was interested in my hand in marriage not for me, but to acquire my father's wealth. That's what his mind was fixed on."

"Mrs. Van Brunt, what do you think every admirer of yours in these parts was fixed on? I heard you had many. What do you think Brom Bones was fixed on?"

"Mr. Crane, out of all my admirers, Abraham was the only one not focused on my father's wealth, but me. But my personal affairs are not your business. Again, I ask, what is this supposed evidence you have?"

"Your husband tormented my uncle along with his gang of delinquents, vandalized his schoolhouse. I heard your husband even trained some scoundrel dog to follow him about and whine every time he spoke. Brom Bones, your husband, bragged that 'he would double the schoolmaster up and lay him on a shelf of his own schoolhouse.' Mrs. Van Brunt, on the night after my uncle's disappearance, supposedly taken by this imaginary horseman, your husband saw the local blacksmith. Why don't you ask your husband about that?"

"I don't have to, Mr. Crane. I know why he was there."

Julian smiled. "I always can tell when someone lies to me. Have a good day, Mrs. Brunt."

Katrina watched him. Her expression of solidarity with her husband changed to doubt. Sounds of commotion grew in the streets, and she ran out to the main street.

It was about to begin.

One of the Van Brunt barns was turned into a convalescent room for Dutch and his men. It was wide open, with just enough light, and airy, but when it was closed up, it could keep in the heat well. The doctor exited the structure with a black bag in hand to a waiting Mr. Jansen and Mrs. De Paul.

"How are they Mr. Tennant?" Jansen asked.

"Five of the men suffered severe concussions, and two of them were lucky to have been knocked out cold and spared the beating the rest received. They will all survive their injuries, and with simple rest, they'll make a full recovery."

"How could this happen?" Mrs. De Paul asked. "Mr. Dutch is Mr. Van Brunt's top man."

"If I can be presumptuous, sometimes the top man can be the most careless because he starts believing everyone telling him that he's the best."

"Such a savage attack must be answered for," Jansen said.

"And your employer has set out to do just that, though I fear my services will not be needed for the aftermath of the encounter between them and this man calling himself the late Ichabod Crane's nephew. No, I fear that the undertaker's services will be the ones needed."

"I hope this bad business will be over after today," De Paul said.

"We all do," the doctor answered. "Sleepy Hollow and Tarry Town can do without this kind of excitement." He checked his medical bag again. "I have done all I can for the men."

"We'll follow your instructions for care exactly," De Paul added.

"Yes, I know you will. Though I feel their pride will be more wounded than their bodies."

"Then that damage is considerable," Jansen said. "Based on the bloodied and blackened state they were in when they were hauled here, but I suspect you are correct, knowing Mr. Dutch as we do."

"We'll have your horse brought 'round, Mr. Tennant," Mrs. De Paul said as she motioned to one of the field boys.

The boy nodded and ran to the adjacent barn.

The two head servants walked with the doctor as the field boy appeared again with a brown horse in tow.

"Thanks again, doctor," De Paul said.

"You are both welcome."

"Mr. and Mrs. Van Brunt would be here themselves to thank you personally," Jansen said.

"Yes, I know they are already in Tarry Town. I most likely will see them on my way back."

Mrs. De Paul noticed something in the barn and called the field boy back.

"Willie?"

"Yes, Mrs. De Paul."

"Where's the new pony?"

The field boy looked as he ran closer to the barn. His

head bobbed left and right as he looked around.

"I don't see him, Mrs. De Paul." He turned to another field boy. "Where's Gremlin?"

"Gremlin?"

"The new pony."

"He was right there in that stable before."

"He's not there now."

Both boys looked around together.

"Mrs. De Paul, we don't know where the pony could be. No one else rides him so no one would have taken him."

"Oh no!" Mrs. De Paul yelled out in panic.

De Graaf stood in the center of the road with a worried look on his face as they came. A cloud of dust followed the approaching riders. He counted at least two dozen before the image of the lead rider came into focus—a determined Brom Bones. His hand rose and the posse came to a stop about a foot from the man.

"Mr. Van Brunt, please. Please don't do this. The town council knows your quarrel with this stranger is legitimate. We only ask that you wait for the marshal to arrive and then we do this in a lawful way. This is not the old frontier days when we made up the law as we went. We're a civilized town now. The stranger isn't going anywhere. Let's wait for the marshal."

"Why? Before we got to town, I was told that this supposed Julian Crane is in fact a marshal himself, and we all know they'll probably stick together like thieves and I won't get any kind of justice from the law."

"Mr. Van Brunt, we have big things planned for these parts, you and I. We are past this kind of behavior. Wait for the marshal, and you'll have everyone's support in Tarry Town, including mine."

"I know you evacuated the town. You are predictable in your efficiency. He lies, accuses me of crimes, steals my men's horses and now he's savagely beaten my men and strung them up to hang from Major Andre's Tree. The marshal isn't here, but I am. Get out of the way, or we will ride over you."

De Graaf quickly moved to the side as the posse galloped past.

"Find him," Brom yelled.

The riders fanned out through the town. Brom remained sitting on his horse, a gun in each hand, in the center of the main road. It was not his favorite horse, but this one would do.

Inside the main store, the Elders watched the posse scatter throughout the town with Mrs. Van Brunt beside them.

"Mrs. Van Brunt, you shouldn't have come into town," Mr. Boer said. "This is going to be bad."

"I had to try one last time to stop what we know is about to happen," she said.

"These two men have to tangle," another elder said. "It has to happen. No point gettin' in the way anymore to try to stop it."

"Why, Mrs. Van Brunt?"

The low voice came from a tiny woman who stood behind them in the store with distressed eyes.

"Why? What do you mean, Mrs. Bakker?" Katrina asked as the men looked on.

"The Headless Horseman hasn't been seen nor heard for some ten years. We haven't even spoken its evil name.

Now you all make it a center of full conversation again."

"None of this is my doing, Mrs. Bakker, or my husband's. It is this stranger who has caused all of this unrest. He almost killed my husband's men, and he spends his time spreading spurious lies about my husband with no hint of evidence."

"You don't even understand. None of you do. This isn't about two mortal men at war with each other. We're tempting the spirits. The war is between our mortal souls and evil, dark forces. We made it go away because we did not speak its name, and it let us be for ten years. Now doubters come into our town, doubting its power, doubting its evil. You're going to make it come back, all of you! You're going to make the Horseman come back!"

Mrs. Bakker was terrified. That fear was transferred to everyone else in the store. Katrina swallowed hard.

Hans continued to chop his wood for the fireplace. He didn't need to anymore. He had plenty to last for weeks, so it was more habit to pass the time. Today he did it to try to keep his mind off of other things, but it wasn't working. He stopped and stood up to look in the direction of Tarry Town. He knew what was about to happen, but there was nothing for him to do about it.

He liked Julian as much as he had liked Ichabod. He didn't want his new acquaintance to end up like his old friend. Julian didn't have room in his skeptical head to believe in the Horseman or any supernatural being, but Hans forgave him for that. He just didn't want Julian to end up like Ichabod in the end, dead, and be permanently remembered with an adjective attached to his name forever.

That poor Mr. Ichabod Crane.
That poor Mr. Julian Crane.

Several of the riders split away from the main group and rode at breakneck speed to the edge of the town. At each end, three sentries were already stationed to stand watch and stop anyone from leaving. The other riders quickly tied up their horses and marched down the street. No matter how long it took, the posse was to check every building, every room, every corner, and every possible hiding place to find Julian Crane.

Brom told them that it didn't matter if he was a marshal. "Get him and we'll sort out the consequences later," Brom said. No one asked what "get" meant. They had already decided amongst themselves that they'd shoot him on sight.

Two men reached the town livery stable and rushed in with guns drawn. They looked at each horse to verify none were the stranger's. One of the men ran up to the second floor to check. The remaining man, when done with inspecting the horses, ran back outside to circle the entire building.

Another two men reached the church.

"He's not here," the pastor said to them in a disgusted voice.

"We'll check anyway," said one of the men.

"Do what you will," he said back as they brushed past him. "Interesting that looking for a man to kill is the only way to get you in these walls."

"When I die, you have my permission to bring me in these walls," one of the men said back sarcastically.

The men walked down the aisles looking at each empty

pew before searching the rest.

Tarry Town's schoolhouse main door was barricaded. The men who reached it didn't bother to force it. They looked through the windows to see all the children sitting on the floor watching them.

The stern schoolmaster gestured them away with his hands. "Go away from here! Don't you bring no gun fighting near the children!" he yelled at them.

Several men made a search of the taverns, and more checked each establishment as they walked up and down the street. De Graaf made himself as visible as possible to try to keep both Brom's men from going too far in disrupting the people's business and to keep the townspeople calm by showing there was at least some kind of impartial authority on the street to look after things.

Julian's horse was tied up in front of the post office. The three riders walked up slowly with guns raised, everyone in Tarry Town and the Hollow knew what his horse looked like by now. The horse looked up at them and bit at the air as they drew closer.

Nearby they could see an abandoned wagon filled with bales of hay. The first man could see someone hiding in the hay and smiled. He touched his lips with his finger and then pointed to it. The other two men nodded. All three of them pointed and fired.

Brom could hear the shots from his post and could now see all his riders moving to the scene. More shots echoed and then more. He smiled. *The end of Julian Crane.*

"*Get down from your horse!*"

The voice behind him made his heart stop. Brom turned his head slowly and there was the man—Julian Crane—

aiming his gun right at Brom's forehead.

"Get down from your horse! I'm not going to say it again!"

Brom ignored him. The expression on his face was devoid of any emotion. Julian moved closer and gripped his gun with both hands, ready to fire. Brom threw one leg over his horse and jumped down.

"My men will kill you!" he yelled.

"Perhaps, but the one thing I do know is that you shall be the first body for the undertaker this day." Julian kept his gun aimed at Brom's face. "This is it for you, Brom Bones. You chased my poor uncle down in the middle of the night and killed him. It was a cowardly crime to get him out of your way to allow you to marry the daughter of the richest man in town. My uncle was a man who never did you no wrong. And you murdered him!"

"I didn't kill him! He was full of life when I left him. I scared him, yes. Chased him, yes. Threw a stupid pumpkin at him, yes. But I didn't kill him!"

"I'm sending you to hell. Good-bye, Mr. Brom Bones."

Julian aimed and Brom felt his knees buckling.

Time slowed down in Brom's eyes. He saw himself as a youngster barely reaching up to his father's knees. He saw himself as a rough-and-tumble, bold and brash young man with his Sleepy Hollow Gang following his every step on their never-ending misadventures in around the Hollow. He remembered when he first saw Katrina—how beautiful she was. He remembered standing before Old Man Van Tassel in a borrowed suit, standing as erect as he could, to formally ask permission for her hand. His future father-in-law was noticeably impressed with him in following the traditional ways. He didn't have to ask him for permission, as Katrina would make up her on mind in this matter. He did anyway, and the Old Man smoked his pipe in satisfaction at the show of deference. He remembered the feeling when Katrina answered, "Yes." He saw their wedding again. He felt the immense joy in his heart, and only one other event in his life could rival such a feeling. His entire life was playing before his eyes.

In an almost inaudible whisper, but to Julian, it was the loudest sound he had ever heard, Brom looked at him with sad eyes and said to this earthly agent for the Grim Reaper, "I didn't kill him."

Julian's finger paused on the trigger.

"Don't kill my father! You, bad man!"

Julian was beginning to turn when Brom yelled out, "Peter!"

A blur ran past Julian and a child jumped in front of his father with his hands outstretched. "You shall not kill my papa!" Brom grabbed him by the collar of his shirt and put the boy behind himself. "You're a bad man!" The boy popped out again from behind his father. "You shoot my papa and I'll get you, you bad man!"

The little boy was probably around five years old. There he was trying to protect his father with defiance, but there was also a growing panic in his face. The boy knew what death was, and he was terrified that it was about to happen to his father.

Julian holstered his gun. The two men stared at each other. Peter clutched his father's leg tightly and his eyes started to tear up from fear, praying that the gun wouldn't be pointed at his father again.

In the distance, Julian saw Mrs. Van Brunt running to them as fast as her legs could move. Off to the side was a cute brown pony that he imagined the boy rode all by himself into town. Several people ran close behind her, including Mr. De Graaf. Julian looked up at Brom one last time and then walked back the way he came.

Katrina grabbed her son into her arms. "Peter! Peter, how could you do such a thing?"

"Mama, I had to keep that bad man from killing my papa!"

She held him tight. "Yes, you did."

Brom realized that he was holding his breath. He inhaled deeply as he bent down and grabbed his knees. The other riders reached them and watched Julian in the distance.

"Mr. Van Brunt, we'll run him down," one of them said.

"Let him be," Brom said.

He stood and couldn't stop hugging his wife and son both. Katrina looked into his eyes, and they both had tears. He had stared across the threshold of death and was shaken to his soul by the experience.

"What do you want us to do, Mr. Van Brunt?" one of men asked.

"Send the riders home. It's over."

Follow

"Come with me!"

Six months ago Julian had met the man.

"Sleepy Hollow is where I am going," Julian answered.

He had been through so many towns that they were starting to run together in his mind along with all the people he had encountered. But he would never forget the bizarre animals, the feeling of dread, and the nightmares, even though he tried to convince himself that he had. And there was a man whose encounter stayed with him from when he passed through the northernmost part of Virginia on his way back from both Tennessee and Kentucky.

It was a tiny town. He expected to be in Pennsylvania the next day on his way to New York, and stopped to cautiously ask around what the reputation of the Hollow was in surrounding areas. Almost everyone knew it for its tales of ghosts. The more sober folk said it was a nice place to visit.

"Why don't you tell me why you're going there?" the man asked.

He was wearing deerskin clothes with a black hat. He

never met a Black Indian before and learned he was part Mohawk, which normally meant to Julian that he wouldn't be friendly. But the War was over, and they were all one nation now.

Somehow the man managed to get Julian's true intentions out of him. It seemed that the man already knew what they were before Julian revealed them. They sat in a local eatery where the man told Julian all about Sleepy Hollow in more detail than anyone had recounted for him before along his long journey.

At one point, he grabbed Julian's hand. The Indian's skin was fully callused and one of the little fingers on his left hand was gone. He explained to Julian that a coyote wanted it more than he did when the Indian was a toddler. The man had grabbed Julian's hand to ensure Julian paid close attention.

"Don't go to Sleepy Hollow," the man said.

Julian smirked. "I've been traveling for half the year and planning for the half year before that. Sleepy Hollow will be seeing me in three days and that's all there is to it. Not you nor anyone else will be stopping me."

"Don't go to Sleepy Hollow," the man warned him again. "It will be a road to evil that you will not be able to pull yourself from once you start. At the end of that road will be true evil."

The man knew his breath was wasted. He even tried to scare Julian with talk of dark clouds following Julian and that he was entering a world where evil did not want him to go.

Julian laughed. "I don't believe any of that superstitious, supernatural nonsense."

The Indian chose not to be offended.

As the evening drew on, with plenty of drink in his belly, the man started to tell a tale.

"There's a story among my people about a great brave. He was the greatest warrior who had ever lived. But as with most great heroes, he had a fatal flaw. There also existed a great black buffalo, and it was the most fearsome beast that had ever lived in the lands. Its soul was as black as its fur and its eyes. It killed many braves and wounded many more. It even killed the great brave's family.

"The great brave said he would kill the beast, and despite the wisdom of the elders, he refused help from any of the tribes in his great hunt. It became his obsession, and that would be the great brave's undoing. He thought because he was the strongest and most capable hunter that he needed no one, that revenge would be his alone. He left his tribe to hunt the great black buffalo alone, saying he could not allow anyone else to share the danger with him. He said these words not out of bravery and concern for his people, but of vengeful hubris. He alone would bring back the bones of the great black buffalo, he declared to all.

"Many moons passed and the great brave never returned. A scouting party was finally sent out to find him.

"The great brave had found the great black buffalo. He had hunted it to the ends of the great cliff. The brave avenged himself on the buffalo as he professed. Never surrendering to fear.

"They found both of them at the bottom of the great cliff. He had speared the beast to death, and it had gored him to death. They went to the great cliff to fight, and both went over the cliff in death, side by side for all eternity in a lake of blood made from them both. The brave never listened to his people. There was no reason for him to die. The beast was clever and ran until the great brave had exhausted himself. It knew the brave would never give up his pursuit. It took advantage of the brave's obsessive hate.

"There is nothing great about lying broken and dead at the bottom of a cliff with a rabid animal next to you, Julian Crane. Especially when that is not how the gods intended for your life to end. Sometimes self-sacrifice is not the bravest path after all. Sometimes a great brave must work with others, not because he's not brave but because that bravery can so easily be confused with many base emotions that are far less noble. Sometimes the bravest thing to do is...simply walk away."

Julian had been quiet all along as the Black Indian told his story. The two of them were sitting across from each other in a tiny tavern with large glasses in front of them.

"I hope the moral of my story isn't lost on you. Intelligent people are often the least wise people when it comes to what really matters in life."

The man took a last gulp from his glass before leaving without even a good-bye.

Julian realized that it was doubt that made him remember this man from so many months ago. Had he made the right decision after all? Was his "hunt" a folly from the start? Who killed his poor uncle then, if not Brom? What would he do now?

Julian didn't bother to go back for his horse. He would do that later tonight. He walked the two miles back to the Hollow and then to Van Ripper's place. It was the only friendly place left to him.

"What are you plannin' to do now?" Hans asked him.

Julian sat at his supper table with a cup of coffee in hand. Hans sat across from him with his own cup.

"I don't know."

"I thought you said you were gonna hunt that foul murderer of your uncle Ichabod Crane to the ends of the earth if need be."

"I was. I am."

"What happened then?"

"Brom didn't kill him."

"You were so certain before that he did it."

"I have a talent for seeing through lies. Brom didn't do it."

"What made you so certain before?"

"What does it matter? My conclusions were false."

"I told you who killed your uncle, but you chose to disregard me. I knew Ichabod better than you."

"I know, but I will stick with the murderers of the natural world before I start looking for those in the supernatural one."

Hans leaned back. "I think you owe Brom an apology for the trouble you caused him. If you are sure he didn't do anything foul to your uncle, after all."

"I don't need to do that. We understand each other. Nothing more needs to be said."

"Is that so?" Hans smiled and stood from the table. "Are you leaving Sleepy Hollow?"

"I don't know yet. I need to rethink my plans."

"Yes, I'd say you have to do a lot of improvement in that arena."

"Hans, when was the last time this Headless Horseman was seen by anyone in Sleepy Hollow or nearby?"

"Ten years ago, I suppose."

"After my uncle disappeared?"

"Yes, I suppose."

"Why do you think that's the case?"

"There's nothing to think. It was satisfied with all the souls and Hollow blood it got."

"I thought your boogieman wanted heads not blood."

"Take a man's head off his body and, believe me, there's plenty of blood."

Julian felt himself starting to laugh but held it back. "I can't argue with that."

They could hear commotion outside the cabin—horses riding up, and men talking and walking up to the door.

There was a knock, and Hans walked to the front door. He noticed Julian slowly remove his gun from the holster and hold it under the table. Hans shook his head at him in disapproval.

"Hans!" A man in a tan cowboy hat stood at the opened door.

He was very tall with a large mustache and stubble for a beard. His long tan coat almost touched the ground and wasn't buttoned, and one could see a glimpse of his gun belt underneath.

His eyes caught Julian at the table. "There you are." He turned back to Hans. "Are you going to let me in, or am I going to have to stand out here for a hundred years?"

Hans let the man enter the cabin. It looked like at least a dozen riders were with him, but they made no movement to dismount.

The man walked to Julian and extended his hand. "Mr. Julian Crane, I am United States Marshal Damian Marshall."

"United States Marshal Julian Crane."

The Marshal grinned as he glanced at Hans. He turned back to Julian and his chin rose. "You mean specially appointed Marshal Julian Crane? You're in the job for revenge. I'm in the job to maintain law and order. You don't mind if I read that letter you have from the governor that I've been told about."

Julian reached in his coat and handed him the letter. The Marshal read it slowly. "I doubt Governor Jay would've signed this had he known he was empowering a vigilante." He handed it back to him.

"The Governor and I are friends. He knew what he was signing."

"Mr. Crane, a whole lot of folk told me what happened today and what could have happened today all because of you and what you set into motion. Can you explain yourself?"

"There's nothing to explain. My uncle Ichabod Crane was murdered and I'm hunting the murderer."

"Ichabod Crane murdered? That schoolmaster who supposedly disappeared from the Hollow about a decade ago? Why do you say he was murdered?" the Marshal asked.

"'Cause he was," Julian snapped back.

The Marshal looked to be stifling a chuckle. Julian's eyes narrowed, wondering what was so amusing to the lawman.

"Ichabod Crane isn't murdered, Marshal Crane. He's alive and well," the Marshal said.

"Alive?" Julian couldn't believe his ears.

"Ichabod's alive," Hans repeated, as shocked as Julian.

"Yes, I saw him."

Julian jumped up from his chair. "Saw him?"

The Marshal continued, "Yes, maybe six months ago. Is that what all this trouble is about? Why you were gonna kill Mr. Van Brunt, a leading member of this town, and why he was gonna kill you?"

"Why wouldn't you have told anyone such a thing?" Hans asked.

"He promised me to secrecy, but under the circumstances...Well then, let's put an end to all this foolishness. Get your things and get your horse, Marshal Julian Crane. I'll take you to your uncle to see for yourself. Though, I suspect that either you or Mr. Van Brunt will try to kill him for real for putting folks through all this chaos in the streets."

Part II
The Marshal

Omen

"Follow me to Ichabod Crane, see!"

Damian Marshall was the U.S. Marshal for the region going on seven years. It was something that the local townspeople were proud of. He had a good reputation and did not drink or carouse around like many of his colleagues in nearby townships. It was always about duty with him, and he was also known for his tenacity in tracking down criminals, his objective fairness, and even a tender side. On more than one occasion, he helped a young man get back on the right track in life when he started to stray. Everyone just called him Marshal.

However, Julian noticed that Hans didn't take to him at all. There seemed to be a history between the men but neither would speak of the particulars. It had to do with more than the opposing views of Hans, a true believer in the Horseman, and the Marshall who supposedly often said, "There is no such darn thing as a headless horseman." Julian's sentiments exactly, but he still trusted Hans Van Ripper over any other person in these parts, including the Marshal.

"Marshal Crane, I'm going to get back to town and smooth over all the hot feelings people have over you. I've never seen the good people of Sleepy Hollow develop such a bad disposition towards someone so fast. The only people they hate more are the British Reds and the Indians who sided with them, and you ain't them. You've made a mess of your reputation in these parts for a long time to come."

"It wasn't intentional, Marshal."

The Marshal shook his head. "Maybe you shouldn't have come into this town with your one-man revenge play. We are supposed to be lawmen. How close did you come to killing Mr. Van Brunt?"

Julian looked on without answering.

"As I thought. You do know if that had happened and if Mrs. Van Brunt didn't gun you down right there on the spot, every man in the town, and I do mean every, would have shot you dead in an orgy of violence. And that little piece of paper you have from the Governor would have been as worthless to you as a rabbit with no legs in a den of foxes."

"Marshal, I do understand how bad things could have become today. I have already admitted I was wrong. I'm sorry for all this."

"I sure hope so. I truly hope you are. Get your things and we can get going when I return."

There wasn't anything for Julian to gather together. Everything he owned was in his saddle pack on Caleb Williams. The Marshal rode back to Tarry Town with his men. "We leave at first sunrise," were the last words he said to Julian.

Hans seemed relieved to have him gone from his land.

He moved about his house doing chores, more to pass the time than for a specific purpose. Julian could sense that he was happy to have company and eager to say something, but didn't.

"Mr. Van Ripper, thank you for putting me up here on your property. I hope it will not cause you any trouble in the town."

Hans smiled. "I'm an old man. Only Old Man Van Tassel has been in Sleepy Hollow longer than me. I don't mind them, and they don't mind me. But you're welcome. What do you expect to find on this trip with the Marshal?"

Julian gave him a questioning look.

"Ichabod is dead," Hans said. "And no man did it. I told you that the first day we met and you almost killed an innocent man by your own admission. Now the Marshal rides in here and you're about to ride off again on a—"

"Mr. Van Ripper, a U.S. Marshal tells me that my uncle is alive, knows where he is, and will take me to him. I'm I supposed to say, 'Oh no, Marshal, my uncle Ichabod is dead. He was taken away by the Horseman?'"

Hans thought for a moment. "Yes. You should go."

Julian felt bad about giving offense to the man. "One of two things is going to happen. Either I won't be back as I'll be with my uncle or I'll be back and we'll put together a super posse to hunt down this Horseman of the Hollow."

Hans smiled at him. "I'll see you when you get back then."

The Marshal had Julian promise not leave Hans's property. Emotions were still too high, and though a full-scale shoot-out had been averted, there was no need to tempt chance. Julian occupied his time with writing a letter to his folks. He hadn't seen them in over a year, and he liked to keep them abreast of his adventure-filled life. But Julian finished early and decided to make one stop before his midnight rendezvous.

"The Marshal?"

"Yes, I'm going to have some dealings with him and want to know what kind of man he is," Julian said to the man.

The Tappan Zee was a growing area but it was still small compared to towns he was accustomed to, and he was a city dweller himself. He promised not to wander around Sleepy Hollow or set foot near Tarry Town but that left everywhere else that was in close riding distance. Julian wanted to get additional supplies for the trip, but also get some community references about the Marshal.

"The man is a saint," the man said. "He's been the marshal for these parts for years. I never heard a bad word spoken about him."

"You can count on him to keep the peace. He's a thinking lawman and not quick to shoot. I've seen him calm more situations down by talking than from any gun. He's known for that," said another man.

"Back a couple of years ago, there was a big fire in town and he personally ran in and saved an entire family — man, woman and child."

"Yes," the second man remembered.

"That's what he did without any regard for his own life. He could have gotten burnt up in the fire himself but that didn't stop him from saving that family."

Julian spoke with several other people in Sing-Sing, and all the accounts were the same. The Marshal had a good, solid reputation throughout the region and probably would be its marshal for decades if that was what he wanted. Everyone knew him, from the smallest child to the oldest person.

Hans had lent him his coat and an old hat, which was his only disguise, and he kept off the main road from and back to Han's place. He had gotten back almost two hours ago, and it was time for his last bit of business for the long day.

It was dark and he had to hold his watch piece close to the table lamp to see the time. Julian softly closed the door behind him as he made his way outside by moonlight. He stood on the hill that Brom's man Ayden used to spy on the Van Ripper cabin, just as he was now doing. All he could hear was the occasional sound of crickets and the wind blowing through the trees. With the Sabbath stillness of the night, he could see why Sleepy Hollow was given to all manner of accounts of strange sights and sounds. He personally would never live in such an eerie place.

There it was. He saw the lamp in the distance moving towards him.

"Mr. Crane?" He heard the man's voice before he was in full view.

"Yes. It's not Sleepy Hollow's favorite specter."

"Ha. I hope you didn't have long to wait. It can get especially spooky standing out in a Hollow night all alone. You should have been here at the height of the Horseman's nightly rides as he looked for his head through the countryside and among the graves in the churchyard. There would be times a lone wolf in the hills would give out a howl that would make the hairs of your back tingle. No wolves anymore, though. People move in and the critters move elsewhere. But still, no man should be alone out here at night."

"I'm never alone, Mr. Knickerbocker," Julian said.

"Oh yes, the Good Lord you mean."

"Him, too, but I meant this." He pointed to his gun belt. The man gave a muffled laugh.

"Did you hear what happened in town?" Julian asked.

"Everyone has."

"I came close to gunning down an innocent man in front of his infant son, and it was all set in motion by a letter from you."

Knickerbocker could see Julian's angry look in the moonlight.

"Sorry, Mr. Crane. I can only tell you what I saw and what I heard. Brom Bones rode into the blacksmith's the following night after your uncle disappeared because his horse lost its shoe. He was bragging on how he put an end to that 'rooster neck Ichabod.' He said he'd never be seen again. He said he was buried so far in the ground that he'd never be seen again. The blacksmith asked him if he killed the poor schoolmaster and Brom said emphatically, 'Yes, Mr. Blacksmith, that is what buried so far in the ground so you'll never be seen again, means.'"

"What else?"

"And like I said in the letter, Brom had a look of knowing whenever the subject of Ichabod's demise came up, and he burst out in laughter at the mention of the Horseman's pumpkins. There is nothing else."

"Well Brom Bones didn't kill him. This Marshal said he saw my uncle six months ago and is taking me to him."

"I don't know what to say, Mr. Crane. I told you what I saw and heard. Oh, and Brom said he even killed that mangy horse Ichabod was riding."

"Why didn't you tell me that before?"

Knickerbocker hesitated. "Why is that important? You wanted to know about your poor uncle, not his poor horse."

"That poor horse belonged to Hans Van Ripper, and the horse returned to his cabin after Ichabod disappeared."

The man swallowed hard. "I didn't know that. Hans's horse? I am sorry, Mr. Crane."

"Brom Bones was telling tales to keep up his devious reputation in town."

"Yes, that is what he was doing. I should have thought of that. I guess in my heart I never believed Brom could kill someone like that. I'm sorry."

"I hope that you are. I could have killed a man in front of his wife and child. I'm not here to put an innocent man's blood on my hands."

"But you don't believe in the Horseman?"

"No, I don't believe in any ghost or goblin."

"I am so sorry, Mr. Crane. It was not my intent to cause all this trouble or get Brom killed. He was a big bully to me and anyone not part of his Sleepy Hollow Gang, but I swear I didn't want to see him or anyone killed."

"Forget it. I know you had no malicious intent. I blame myself. I believed what I wanted and did not look any further when I should have."

The man managed a faint smile. "But Mr. Crane, soon you'll be reunited with your long, lost uncle. This will have a happy ending for you after all."

A faraway wolf's howl pierced the silence of the night. The men couldn't help but to glance at one another.

Trek

"Riding we will go! Ichabod, here we come!"

The rabbit dropped lifeless in an instant. The Marshal was a crackerjack shot from even this distance, using a pistol rather than a rifle.

"We got supper," the Marshal said as he stood.

Other than securing the day's food, the only other excitement, if it could be called that, was the two men taking the flatboat to cross the Hudson River. Caleb Williams had done it many times before, but was always feisty when time came to get on a boat for a water ride.

When they rode out of Sleepy Hollow at sunrise, the countryside was both hospitable and inviting. The terrain looked magical with its trees of yellow, orange, and purple leaves. Squirrels were chasing each other up one trunk to another, and small birds were darting from branch to branch. Julian took it as a sign of good things to come for their trip at hand. Maybe that was how it was supposed to be. The land fancied you when you were departing, as you were no longer a stranger. Otherwise, all it had for you were fearful sights and sounds.

Under the night moon, the two men sat around the campfire eating the last portions of meat from their flat metal plates between swallows of coffee. Julian ate with his bare hands. Marshal ate his meal with a hunting knife in each hand, which drew Julian's attention.

"Ever had to use those on anything walking on two legs?" Julian asked.

Marshal pulled a small bone from his teeth. "Many times. You know the life. Days and weeks alone in the wild, with only your horse for company. A hungry bear would be the nicest thing you'd run into. Anyone else and they'd kill you in your sleep to get your horse, your boots, the possessions in your pockets, or because maybe they liked your hat. You never know who's skulkin' about, waitin' to drag you away. We may be lawmen, but there is no law way out here."

"How long have you been marshaling?"

"When did the Act go into effect? 1789? Yes, so I became a U.S. Marshal right from the start. I was a sheriff in Charleston, down in South Carolina, and before that, in the War."

"Whose command were you under?"

"I was under General Washington, the American Fabius himself."

Julian wasn't sure if the latter phrase was praise or scorn. "I was in the War, under Washington, too. Boston, New York, New Jersey. Crossed the Delaware to defeat the Hessians at Trenton. After, his army had to split, so I was assigned to a detachment to protect the Hudson River area. Probably not too far from where we are now."

"I joined him when they marched to Valley Forge."

"You were at Valley Forge?"

Julian perked up to hear more. He had heard many stories of the ordeal and none of it was good. But he never had come across a soldier who could give him a personal and direct account until now. He noticed that the Marshal sat quiet, as if he had to sort through the bad images in his mind until he was able to fashion the appropriate words to follow.

"I was. Thousands of men not cut down by British guns or bayonets but by the elements. Thousands died. Freezing to death in the worst winter cold anyone could remember, succumbing to every manner of disease, and starving to death. We had no supplies, no food. Men walked without even a pair of shoes on, leaving bloody footprints behind in the snow or their rotted off toes."

Julian noticed how Marshal was almost in a trance as he recounted the story.

"The Oneidas helped us there, I was told."

"They brought corn for food. If not for that, we all might have died. We lost nearly half our men and hundreds of our horses before they arrived."

"I can't even imagine the horror," Julian said consolingly.

"For King and country, my childhood friends and I joined the War. Throw off the slave chains of the monarchy to be our own free nation. I remember the speeches well, my friends and I. We eagerly joined the Continental Army, joined Washington just before Valley Forge. How were we to know it would be the worst winter ever recorded? Instead, we found ourselves in an encampment of horrors—disease, cold, filth, death, dead men, dead horses, no one really expecting to survive except the chosen ones. However, for those of us not born with such fortune, one must create it for ourselves in life.

"My first friend died of dysentery. They always invent fancy names or use Latin ones to describe the vile. He died from endless liquid feces passing from his body filled with blood on one end, and endless vomiting from the other end. An infection the dumb doctors called it. He wasted away prostrate in his own filth."

The Marshal looked as he spoke to Julian, but his mind was elsewhere. The memories of his deeds flashed before his eyes. *A pale, gaunt man laid motionless on the ground as a younger Marshal strangles him to death.*

"The doctors used all kinds of words you never heard before or could pronounce if you had to. All a facade for their own ignorance of what killed him, despite all their high medical learning and expertise they claimed to have had.

"My second friend died from typhoid fever. His chest was covered in these reddish spots. No one could comfort him with his nervous fever and headaches. He had no strength to move from his bedroll. The delirium got worse. His fever got so high we thought he might burst into flames."

The sick man's eyes widen as a young Marshal leans down over him and covers the man's mouth. He punches him unconscious before strangling him.

"He died emaciated and broken.

"My third friend died from the flu. Can't remember the fancy medical term for it...yes, influenza. He became a shivering mass from the endless chills of the fever, his nose would never stop running, and there was the coughing. He was also too weak to move and he complained that his muscles ached. The wintry cold only doubled his shivering until one day his shaking stopped, as did every other of his life functions."

The man stares up in fear with his watery, red eyes as a young Marshal pounds the man to death with his fists.

"The Indians came with the food and foreign officers came to train us up into real soldiers. It would be as if Valley Forge never happened. As if none of those men ever died in those horrible ways before their time. All that matters is the higher purpose.

"You see that much death, over and, over. Men's lives become meaningless. They can live or they can die. A death is only to serve the purpose of others. The life of man is not worth anything at all. What does it matter?"

"But that's not true, surely," Julian added.

Marshal came out of his trance and focused. "In war, sometimes you have to think like that or you go insane."

"I know what you mean."

"I did manage to save the lives of some fellow soldiers in battle and get me some commendations and more medals, as if I needed any to begin with."

Julian nodded, impressed. "You were a good man, Marshal."

The Marshal smiled slightly, but didn't respond directly. Soldiers were always shy when it came to praise of their heroics. "You were under General Washington, too?" he asked. "You weren't old enough to be in the War."

"I was a drummer boy. Barely taller than that rabbit we ate. I was with him at the beginning, including those early defeats. The British chased us out of New York. Hit by bullets twice—one knocked my drum right out of my hands and the other grazed my shoulder. But I made it out. A lot didn't. Washington was a fox though. And we have our independent nation. Well, the War is over."

"Until the next one."

"Heard anything about this fighting with the French?"

"I told everyone at the time. The French are not our friends. They just hate the British more, that's why they helped us in the War."

"I heard of this Quasi-War, but it's undeclared and way out at sea, far from here. They attacked us because we were trying to be cordial to the British."

The Marshal looked squarely at Julian to answer. "Not that it matters. It's not here, so why concern yourself with it?"

"I heard the French have good food though." Julian grinned, and Marshal smiled back. "Hopefully, nothing more comes of it."

"You have an interest in the politics. I've never seen a more worthless occupation. Forget the French. We had our revolution against our monarchy, and they had theirs. Neither one of us knows where it will all end up. I have always thought that a man should know his station in life and not go beyond it, know his place and purpose in the world. We're just two marshals out here in the dark world. We're not heads of state, Marshal Crane. Our purpose is getting to your uncle."

Marshal put his metal plate next to his leg and reached into his coat for his tobacco.

"How long will it take for us to get there?" Julian asked.

"We'll leave at sun-up and reach the next town by noon."

"But how long for the whole trip?"

"No more than a week to ten days, I'd say."

"He's been that close all this time? How long will we be in the next town?"

"Don't worry, Marshal Crane. We'll make it to your uncle. My business will take only a few days, and it's all on the way."

Julian was satisfied as he drank from his cup, and the Marshal lit his cigar with a burning stick from the fire.

"The Legend of the Headless Horseman." Julian laughed.

"The Legend of Sleepy Hollow," the Marshal corrected. "That's how it's said. Every secluded town creates its own superstitions. Sleepy Hollow is no different. Gives the people something to talk about and something to scare the children with."

"Why don't you believe in ghosts and goblins, Marshal?"

Marshal looked at him for a moment. "Because I don't."

Julian drank again from his cup. He had the distinct feeling that the Marshal had just lied to him.

The two men broke camp and rode out at sunrise. The early morning was colder than the previous night. Everything green around them had touches of dew as they rode north with the Hudson a quarter mile to their right flank. Julian wondered why they didn't ride close along the riverbank.

"Why does your horse have two names like it was a human being?" Marshal asked.

"Caleb Williams is a human being," Julian joked as he stroked his horse's mane. "What's the name of yours?"

"Body Snatcher."

The small talk between the men was light, and the ride was easy and uneventful as they made their way to town. The Battle of Stony Point under Mad General Anthony Wayne happened near this town of Waynesburg. Everywhere they rode or walked was some part of the new nation's history.

As they neared the town, Julian noticed the presence, in significant numbers, of Negroes. However, none of them seemed to be there on their own accord. He realized that he hadn't seen one in the Tarry Town area. Most of the slaves filled wagons either moving into town or out. Despite key abolitionist leaders from the Governor on down and active abolitionist societies, African slave labor had been increasing in the States.

"Quite the impressive place, a paragon of the principles of our new nation. *All men are created equal,*" Julian said.

The sarcasm wasn't lost on Marshal, who gave him a disapproving look.

Other than the slave activity in and around town, it looked like every other New England town to Julian. They reached the sheriff's station and dismounted in unison. It was a solid brick block building that could double as a miniaturized fort if it had to. Julian tied up Caleb Williams to the post and stroked the horse's mane. He saw more than a few wagons of slaves passing by. The Marshal was suddenly right next to him.

"I know that I don't have to tell a fellow lawman that we avoid and defuse confrontations. We don't instigate them."

"You didn't like my commentary?" Julian was about to step away. The Marshal grabbed his arm.

"If you want to be the Patrick Henry of the abolitionist

movement, then do so after we've concluded our business and you and your uncle are off on your way away from me. I got to work with these people every day. You're just passing through. There's a time to fight and a time to keep quiet. Keep your opinions to yourself. Understand? You don't piss in another man's bed. Do you understand, Marshal Crane?"

"I understand."

Marshal let his arm go, and he took the lead to the town sheriff's building.

"Marshal-Marshal!" The man behind a desk jumped up with a smile. "Back so soon." He shook Marshal's hand and patted him on the shoulder.

"Had a change of plans."

"You're welcome anytime, Marshal. Who's your friend?"

"Sheriff, this is my colleague Marshal Julian Crane."

"Hi, sonny." He shook his hand, too. "You're kinda young for a marshal."

"I started when I was two years old," Julian joked. He glanced at the Marshal. "And the Marshal here was telling me outside how I had the perfect disposition for a lawman."

Marshal smirked.

"Yes, our Marshal has a gift for sizing up a man and knowing his strengths and faults. Have a seat, gentlemen."

The Sheriff went back to his seat behind the desk. Marshal and Julian pulled up a couple of chairs from against the wall to the front of the desk and sat.

"Where're your deputies?" Marshal asked.

"Meyer is making rounds, which in his case means he's probably at the pub. De Wit just had a new son, so I gave him the day off to tend to the family. Do you need help with something? Well, you don't need our help anymore. You have your Marshal Crane."

"I'm looking for Frenchie," Marshal said. "I have a warrant for him."

"Frenchie? What'd he do now?" the Sheriff asked.

"Murder," Marshal answered flatly.

The Sheriff shook his head, but he didn't seem all that surprised. "We haven't seen him. Last time was…'round the time you were last here."

"Spread the word that I'm looking for him. We'll be here today and then poke around in town the next day before ridin' out. He always stays in the area, so if I miss him this time, I'll get him on the way back," Marshal said.

"I'll notify my deputies." The Sheriff grabbed his hat from the corner of his desk. "Let's walk down to the pub for a meal."

"You can tell me who Frenchie is," Julian added.

The door flew open and one of his deputies ran in. He immediately noticed the Marshal. "Marshal, thank God you're here, too!"

"What's wrong?" the Sheriff asked.

The deputy answered, "There's a warpath of Indians headed this way, Sheriff! With rifles. Thousands of them. They'll massacre the entire town!"

Detour

"Let's go by Ichabod another time."

No matter how big a town became or how sophisticated and civilized its people felt they were, all of it was no more than a stone's throw from sheer panic and lawlessness. Men hastily constructed a barricade on the main road into town, while others were boarding up all windows of the buildings. Women gathered all children and headed to the church in the center of town that was being remade into a fortress.

Others, most of them visitors, were doing the opposite. They were gathering their belongings as fast as they could to get out of town. All the slave traders had already cut out for points in every direction. However, any town of greater size and safety was more than forty miles away.

"We can never seem to get away from the killin'," the Sheriff had said aloud in frustration before sending his men off to secure the town and get ready to ride.

The Sheriff may not have been as efficient as Tarry Town's Mr. De Graaf, but they did their best. All places of business were closed, women and children were indoors, and all excess able-bodied men, beyond those needed to protect homes and businesses, were assembled in groups on the main streets to protect the town.

It was all reminiscent of Tarry Town making preparation for Julian's one-man warpath against Brom Bones. Julian still felt shame in the pit of his stomach. He would never have been able to forgive himself if he had killed the man in front of his family. The Marshal's words were correct. They were lawmen, and lawmen were supposed to behave in a certain way, not in any way they pleased.

He thought of the different people of Sleepy Hollow and wondered if he would see them again. He was still a bit sore at Knickerbocker, though he had no reason to be. He wondered what Hans was doing that moment. It was fitting that he was Ichabod's Executor of Estate. Ichabod was the epitome of gregariousness, while Van Ripper was the most crotchety, old man you could ever meet, but he noticed that the man was always friendly towards him. Ichabod was their mutual bond, and that made them a kind of family themselves. He also thought of Katrina Van Brunt and how he wished he could apologize to her in the sincerest way he could manage. Their son was just a child and probably had already forgotten the whole incident with his father being alive and well. Brom and he did understand each other. It was a terrible mistake, people were injured, but no one was killed. But he still wanted to apologize to him directly.

Maybe he would have a chance to do so, but perhaps he was making more of it than he should. That chapter of his life was over. The next one would be the important one: to be united with his dear Uncle Ichabod. That funny looking man whose appearance and smile could send a child into a fit of laughter. Julian smiled to himself and wondered how meeting the man only once in his life as a young boy could leave such an unwavering determination in him these many years later to either find out that his uncle was alive and well or destroy the man who removed him from this earth.

"The troops are already at the fort waiting," the Sheriff said as he led Marshal and Julian through the crowds, all men on horseback. "We have plenty of ammunition in town, but the problem is the lack of men who can shoot straight."

"Are these U.S. soldiers? Any with soldiering experience?" Marshal asked.

"No, all reserves, men from town. I'm one myself," the Sheriff answered.

"Sheriff," called out a man in the lead of a half-dozen riders. He stopped in front of them. "Fort Clinton is sending a detachment. We'll make our stand there."

"How many men do you think we'll have?" the Sheriff asked.

"At least a hundred."

"Hope that's enough," said one of the deputies.

"Did you hear what caused the warpath?" the Sheriff asked.

"No, Sheriff. We don't even know which tribe it is."

"Don't we have treaties with the Five Nations?" Julian asked.

All the men looked at him.

"He's from the city," Marshal said.

"Who are you, mister?"

"U.S. Marshal Julian Crane."

"Well, Marshal Crane, just because we have treaties with them doesn't mean all abide by it. The Iroquois Confederacy isn't one tribe. It's many. Some nice, and some not so nice."

"I betcha a solid silver coin that the British are stirring them up so they can attack America again," another man said.

"Did you hear that rumor about French navy ships firing on us?"

"I thought they were our allies?" another man asked.

"Tell them that. The British, French, Indians. We'll be at war with the whole lot of them before too long," a third man added.

"Let's save the idle chatter for another time," the Sheriff interjected. "Marshal Crane, will you be joining this 'war dance' of ours?"

"Sheriff, point me where you need me to be."

The Sheriff nodded approvingly. "Good man. Gentlemen, let's get moving before the fighting starts without us."

The plains were filled with riders all heading to Fort Clinton. There was no central authority. Men just heard that Indians were coming, U.S. soldiers were en route, and every able-bodied gun was needed to protect the region.

Julian looked out across the plain at the assortment of men—small and large, tall and short, novice and expert—that had responded to the call to fight and protect. The behavior of men could often leave one disillusioned, but then there were times like these that made one proud to be a member of mankind.

The two men were riding by themselves at the moment.

"Why don't you forget about your uncle?" Marshal said. "I told you he's alive. You know he's living well. After all this, you can just ride on back where you're from and live well-off, too."

"Marshal, let's be clear here. My uncle Ichabod isn't alive until I see him with my own eyes and we sit together and trade adventures the whole weeklong. Until then, my uncle is as imaginary as the Headless Horseman. And I shall never stop until I see my dear uncle. Nothing on this earth will deter me. After we're finished with this, are you taking me to him?"

"I always do what I say. I said I'd take you to him, and I will."

"Good, because he's either alive and well, or he's dead and there is a foul murderer to be dealt with."

"Yes, the people of Sleepy Hollow had the misfortune of seeing that part of your blood oath."

"I'm ashamed about that, but not why I did it. I will make deadly sure I'm right next time. But then, that will never happen. You will be taking me to him."

"At our first chance, we'll get away," Marshal said.

They rode quietly for a bit. Julian looked around the plains, confused, realizing they were riding away from the group.

"I thought we were joining the Sheriff and the militia?" Julian asked.

"They have plenty of men. If we don't go now, we could be bogged down here for weeks. Indians are a lot smarter than us. They don't come all at once when they fight. They scatter, confuse, back-track, and circle 'round."

"I think we need to stay with your friend, even if it's out of fellow lawman courtesy. You said so yourself. You have to work with these people. We help him today, and he helps us tomorrow."

Marshal smirked. "Do you want me to take you to your uncle or not?"

Julian stopped his horse. "A day or two or a week is going to make a difference? If my uncle is alive and well, he will be so no matter when we get there. Or is there something more?"

Marshall ignored him. "We'll get there when we get there then."

"Then let's help your friend, the Sheriff."

The day camp was sprawled across the plains. U.S. soldiers had already organized most of the camp, but more riders were always arriving. The Sheriff led both the Marshal and Julian to the commanding officer and introduced everyone.

A scout rider barreled into camp toward the colonel.

"Colonel, the warpath is within eyeshot."

"Major," the Colonel yelled at a group of waiting soldiers in the camp. "Four men with me and have the rest of the troops mounted and ready. We will approach from their flank."

"Colonel," the Sheriff interrupted. "We can accompany you."

"Are you sufficiently armed?" the Colonel asked.

"Guns, rifles, and as much ammunition as our horses can carry," the Sheriff answered.

"Mount up and join my men then," the Colonel said.

Most of the militia was already on their horses, forming a line as the Colonel, his four soldiers, the Sheriff, and the marshals rode to the front. At the hill, everyone saw them.

The Indians were riding northeast slowly. All of them

were in traditional dress, mostly animal hides, bright colors, and in moccasins; a couple of men had boots. There were only a few able-bodied men in the lead. More than half were old people, women, and children. None of them were holding weapons and there was no hostile demeanor about them.

The Colonel looked at his soldiers. "Warpath?"

"Colonel, that's what we were told," the soldier answered, sheepishly.

"Get down there and find out what's happening," the Colonel directed.

"Is it safe, sir?"

"Maybe the little children will attack you and scalp you. Get down there!"

The soldier rode off to the approaching group of Indians. The Colonel raised his right hand and waved slowly to and fro. They could see the Indian at the front of their party do the same back at them. They watched the soldier reach them and ride along the side. After a moment, he headed back.

Marshal didn't even wait for the soldier to return before he gave Julian a disapproving look as he slowly shook his head.

"Colonel." The soldier stopped his horse in front of them. "Oneidas. They were attacked and now are heading to Fort Clinton for safety. The Lakotas are the ones on the warpath. They have been attacking other pro-America Iroquois tribes. There are only about two dozen of them though, but they are well-armed."

"Lakotas? They're a ways east from where they're supposed to be. Not the Mohawks or Senecas? They were the ones who fought on the side of the British," the Major said.

"They said it was the Lakotas, and they described them well."

"This all changes things," the Colonel said. "Major."

"Yes, sir?" the soldier next to him answered.

"We need to do something, Colonel," Julian interjected. "We have to protect them."

"Marshal Crane, we do know how to do our jobs here," the Colonel said with his eyes narrowed.

He watched Julian for a bit. Julian knew it was the man's way of telling him to shut up. The Colonel turned to his men.

"Inform the militia of the news, and tell them that we are going to give them an escort and send some soldiers ahead to let the fort know they are coming," he said.

"Right away, sir," the Major answered.

The Sheriff smiled. "Indians attacking Indians and Indians going to our forts for protection."

"Why shouldn't they?" Julian said. "The Iroquois fought on our side. If it wasn't for Indian help, we wouldn't have survived Valley Forge."

"This feud between the Iroquois and Lakotas is our fault anyway," Marshal added. "We supplied the Iroquois and encouraged them to make war on them and any other tribe in their way and ours. It's payback time now."

"Let's not make more of this than it is," the Sheriff said. "These tribes were fighting and killing each other long before the White man ever set foot on this land at Jamestown."

Colonel turned to his soldiers. "Lieutenant, you ride point with them until they get to the Fort. Ensigns, you two ride ahead to the fort, but take care. Lakotas may send their own riders ahead for an ambush. We think there is bad blood between America and Britain and between Britain and France. It's not even close to the bad blood between these Indian tribes. Sheriff, you can go back to your town and tell them that hell isn't riding into town today. Marshal Crane?"

"Yes, Colonel?"

"Did I forget anything?" he asked sarcastically.

Julian sighed. "Sorry, Colonel. My mother always said I was a willful boy with a large mouth like my uncle. Only he used his for eating, and I used mine for talking." He smiled. "You don't have to say it. The Marshal already told me to be more like my uncle."

The Colonel laughed. "I was a willful boy myself. How else could I become an officer? Sorry, marshals that we got your hopes up. No warpath, just families moving out of harm's way, just like we would have done."

"We'll make our good-byes here," the Sheriff said.

Marshal said, "I'll try to find Mr. Frenchie before I reunite my comrade here with his long, lost uncle."

"Frenchie?" the Colonel asked.

"I know what you're thinking, Colonel. Frenchie, not the French," Sheriff said.

"Yes, I know him," the Colonel revealed.

"There's a bounty on him for murder," Marshal added.

"Murder?" The Colonel was surprised.

"I'm to take him in to stand trial," Marshal said.

The Colonel looked at his soldiers and saw them listening to every word. "We're not having a conversation with you! Go!"

The soldiers raced off in different directions to carry out their orders.

"Marshall, I know where he is, but I find that charge hard to believe," the Colonel said.

"I can appreciate that. He's a popular trader, lots of friends, but you and I both work for the U.S. government and swore an oath of office to follow the laws of this land. The man was accused of a crime. He will have his day in court, judged by his peers and adjudicated by a judge. What he can't do is pick which warrants he will obey and skip town because he views a lawfully executed warrant an inconvenience. The murder was also particularly ferocious—decapitation and mutilation."

Everyone, including Julian, was equally alarmed by the information.

"Decapitated and mutilated?" Sheriff repeated.

"If he's innocent," Marshal continued, "then he'll prove it in court. Unless, Colonel, you're advocating the defiance of this nation's laws."

"No, Marshal, I'm not."

"So someone tell me, where's Frenchie?"

The Marshal leaned back on his horse and folded his arms, looking at them.

Distant Shadow

*"I believe it's following.
Not the main devil, but his little henchmen."*

Marshal took point, and Julian followed as they galloped down the ridge. They moved alongside the convoy of soldiers and Indians. Fort Clinton had played an important role in the War, but it had fallen into a bit of disrepair. Julian touched the tip of his hat in respect when his eyes met the Oneida chief at the front of the trail of horses. He was equivalent to a military general in the American army, but this chief, who smiled and nodded back, had an unassuming demeanor, deceptively so, as these men didn't rise to their honored position for lack of skills, courage or cunning. Julian was a bit surprised that the Marshal ignored not just the chief but also all the Indians despite their tribe's role in saving his life and other Americans at Valley Forge.

After a few miles, Marshal and Julian took a fork in the path, continuing northwest as the main Indian convoy continued north. Julian waved to their sole soldier escort.

"Good luck, marshals," the soldier said as he rode

forward to the head of the convoy.

"We'll get there in about an hour," Marshal said to Julian without being asked.

It was more silent riding for the men. It was not out of unfriendliness towards one another but heightened watchfulness. The soldiers thought they knew exactly where the Indian war party was, which may or may not be the true reality of things.

A shot!

They stopped the horses and scanned the countryside in the direction of the gunshot.

"Not far at all," Julian said. Both men waited for another shot or commotion of any kind. "We should ride to it."

Marshal smirked. "We should ride away from it. Marshal Crane, is this how you do your work? You run to gunfire?"

"Someone could be in trouble."

"Or someone could be baiting us into a trap."

"You stay then, and I'll see what it is about." With that, Julian rode off hard.

He wasn't foolhardy. He stayed close to trees and brush. His gun was already in hand. He jumped down from Caleb Williams when he felt he was closing in on the source of the shot.

A covered wagon was crashed up against a tree! Then he saw the silhouette of a man near a tree across from it a few feet away. The man looked in his direction, turned, and ran off into the forest.

Julian ducked down low as he moved to the wagon. Another man's face popped out from behind it.

"You thieves can come on in if you want, but we got six

gun hands in here and we're prepared to send you and your buddy to hell!" a man yelled out.

"This is Marshal Julian Crane, mister. I heard the shot and came to provide assistance. But if you want me to go, I will."

Julian waited a few moments as he crouched low to the ground. He was worried about the other man who ran off.

"Okay, come on in slow."

Julian rose and walked closer, with his horse blocking their complete view of him. A man will shoot at another man but not a horse, unless the man was some savage, but they didn't sound like savages. At the wagon were two men and a woman, all well dressed. The woman was sitting on the ground, leaning against the wagon, and holding the hand of one of the two men. The other man stood in front of them and only he had a gun. Sprawled on his back lying dead on the ground was a third man, obviously the driver.

"So much for your six gun hands," Julian said.

"Mister, I'm going to have to ask you to prove you are a lawman," the second man directed.

"Important matters first," Julian interrupted. "Where did that other man run off to?"

"How should we know?" asked the first man. "He was the one who ambushed us and killed our driver."

"What kind of barbaric place is this?" the woman screamed. "Whites. Indians. You don't know who's friendly and who will murder you."

Julian pulled his badge from inside his coat pocket and showed it to the three of them.

"Why don't you pin it to the front of your coat like every other legitimate lawman?" asked the other man.

"Because I don't want to give anyone something to aim at," Julian answered as he moved closer to them with his horse in tow.

"What's your name again?" the woman asked.

"Marshal Julian Crane." He returned the badge to his inside coat pocket. "I need you two men to watch that forest. I hardly think that the thief, as you call him, ran off to leave us be. Most likely, he's circling around or waiting for us ahead. We also don't know if there are others with him. Ma'am, I need you to watch my back."

Julian walked over to a side of the wagon and tied up Caleb Williams. He dragged the driver off to the side and inspected the wagon.

"Oh, before I forget, I am not traveling alone. I'm with a fellow lawman."

"You mean him," the second man said.

Julian looked up and the Marshal was slowly riding in.

"I was starting to think you were going to forget about me out of spite," Julian said to him.

"Who's delaying who now? How can I get you to your uncle as quickly as possible if you stop to help every hapless, helpless person or cause you come across?" Marshal said. "Where's the shooter?"

"Ran off into the forest," Julian answered.

"So he can try to back-shoot us or catch us further along."

"Can't do anything about that now. Let's get their wagon fixed and move out of here."

"Where were you all going?" Marshal asked the three people.

"We were heading north as fast as we could," the first man said. "There's a thousand-man army of Indians on the warpath here."

The marshals laughed.

"What's funny?" the man asked.

"There is a group of Indian men, women, and children heading to Fort Clinton," Julian said. "They're fleeing the warpath of Indians, but that warpath is only about two dozen of them."

"Sounds about right. Indians killing Indians. Whites bushwhacking Whites," the second man said.

The wagon was not broken at all. Marshal and Julian pulled it away from the tree with their horses and set it properly. The dead driver was loaded into the back. He would be buried later when and where it was safe.

"We'll ride hard since we don't know where the shooter is," Marshal said. "We can relax when we're in sight of the next town. Can either of you men handle the wagon?"

The second man volunteered. "Yes, I can manage." He showed no fear knowing that he would also have no protection from the shooter as he drove the wagon.

"You ride with them and I'll take the rear," Julian said to Marshal, who nodded.

They were off. Marshal rode hard ahead of the wagon. The wagon followed behind with tremendous speed, sometimes it seemed as if it would tip right over, but the man was an able wagon-driver.

Julian maintained the rear. Something told him to look back, and he did. There he saw the silhouette of a man, in the distance, running after them on foot. Julian stopped Caleb Williams. The man in the distance stopped, too. It was impossible for him to catch them now, but he seemed like he was going to do his best to try. But why? Julian debated whether to just go after him, but he didn't get a chance to decide. The man ran back and disappeared into the trees.

Julian returned to the ride and caught up quickly to his position behind the covered wagon. The wagon passed through the lightly wooded area and was about to head into a denser area of trees when he rode up along the wagon to gesture the driver to slow down and stop.

"What's the matter, marshal?" the driver asked.

"I need to ask some questions," Julian answered.

"Shouldn't we keep moving?" Marshal asked.

The couple in the wagon sat up straight.

"Marshal, what's happening?" the woman asked.

"This man who tried to hijack the wagon, was he on horseback when you first came across him?"

"We never saw him on a horse," the man in the wagon answered. "But we weren't focused on that. He killed our driver, and we were fearful we'd get shot, too. We thought maybe there was a gang of them."

"We didn't even see the man until we settled in behind the wagon, and we only barely saw him then," the woman added.

"Why are you asking, marshal?" the driver asked.

"Yes, why, marshal?" Marshal added.

"This man isn't on a horse now, but he's still running after us. It doesn't make sense."

"He's a criminal and a murderer, marshal. The criminal mind is not one for making sense," the woman said.

"He can't possibly catch us, but he is determined to run after us on foot. Why would he do that? Have you ever seen this man before? Is there something valuable on the wagon?"

"Marshal, what are you suggesting?" the driver asked with a tone.

"I am not suggesting anything. I am simply trying to figure out this criminal. That's what I do, what I'm supposed to do. Also, we may have gotten beyond his grasp, but what about the next victim? Should we leave that victim or victims to this criminal?"

"Marshal, you can't save everyone," Marshal said to him somberly.

"I disagree, Marshal. I don't want to be the lawman who simply shows up after the victim is dead. If I can keep there from being another victim, then I believe that to be part of my duties, too."

The driver changed his attitude and said, "We never saw the man before, marshal, but none of us were able to see his face clearly the first time. He was waiting for us and shot our driver in cold blood."

"And there is nothing valuable on the wagon," the woman said. "You saw all our belongings with your own eyes."

"And even if there were valuables, he wouldn't know about it," the man said. "We loaded up the wagon straight away after we left our hotel."

"I don't doubt any of you," Julian said. "Perhaps he thought you were wealthy or he's targeting every wagon that crosses his path."

Marshal laughed to himself. "Marshal Crane, sometimes things don't have a reason."

"Very true, Marshal, but I look for reasons anyway because most of the time there is a reason. It doesn't mean it's logical or good, but there is one."

"Wish you were this diligent in your thinking when

you first rode into Sleepy Hollow."

"So do I, but that's the past." Julian looked at the driver. "Time to move. Ride as hard as is safe."

"What will you do, marshal?" the woman asked.

"What I need to do. As I said, I believe that if there is a way to stop someone from becoming a victim in the future, to stop someone from making someone a victim, then I have to do that."

The woman smiled at him. "We need an army of lawmen like you, marshal."

The crazy man watched until they became mere dots in the distance. He reappeared from the dense part of the forest, jumping out to continue his run after them.

"I'm gonna get them," he said to himself with a mouth full of rotten teeth. "Get them."

The town was not that far away. Wealthy people like that must have something of value on the wagon, and he would have it.

As he reached another twenty feet, he heard something nearing his heels—fast. He stopped briefly to look back but then turned to run full-speed. He glanced back to see Julian crash through the brush behind him, riding hard.

There was no outrunning him. He stopped, turned, and jutted his head forward as if it were a pouncing cobra.

Julian's whole body jerked back as the man spat a putrid, chunky, black mess from his mouth at him, barely missing his upper body. Julian charged again and as Caleb Williams whipped by, Julian kicked the man hard as he passed.

"You bitch's bastard!" Julian yelled as he turned Caleb Williams around to run at the man again. He checked his clothes and his horse's body to ensure there was no piece of the filthy concoction the vile man had exhaled at them.

But the man was on the ground, face first.

Julian angrily rode to the body. "Get up! I'm taking you in!"

The man remained motionless. Julian jumped down from the horse and kicked the man hard again in his side. No reaction.

It was only after standing there and staring at the man that he realized the shooter was dead.

Julian was a bit disturbed. The kicks were by no means of sufficient force to kill anyone. He turned him over with his foot, and the man's empty eyes stared up at the sky and his bottom lip was covered with black spittle.

Julian leaned down and touched his neck and then his chest. No pulse. No heart beat. Julian stood up again and shook his head.

How could the man just die like that?

A black shape descended into his view and a shot rang out! Feathers exploded in his face.

Julian threw himself back, rolled, and scurried along the ground as fast as he could to prop his back up against a large tree. He shook the panic from himself as he looked where the shot most likely came from. He looked up and saw several circling black birds high above the trees, directly overhead. They made strange calling sounds in unison that sounded almost like hissing. But more important to him were the sounds of someone on horseback riding quickly away.

He glanced around the tree to see the dead man on the ground, in the exact spot and position, but next to the body was a giant black vulture bird—dead, with its feathers everywhere. Julian stayed quiet behind the tree to wait a while. Caleb Williams seemed quite unnerved by the growing number of black birds in the air.

Julian was uneasy by the hellish birds too, but more so by the fact that someone tried to shoot his head off. Only sheer luck and one of the birds inadvertently diving into the bullet's path saved his life.

His mind filled with images of that chunky, black spit from the dead would-be thief.

This region was cursed, not haunted. That's what he always felt. However, now another notion was creeping into his head, especially after that night with Knickerbocker, standing there, and pretending not to be frightened by the howling wolf. Maybe it wasn't the land, maybe it was *him*, like the Black Indian had said. Some invisible, foreboding cloud was following him, and with it came everything that was bizarre, unnatural, and unholy. It was the price to be paid for this quest for his unfortunate uncle.

Who just tried to blow my head off?

Julian knew that the wagon would be safe with the Marshal. Whoever it was that shot at him would not be able to get away if he did so again against the Marshal.

The sounds of the vultures turned to frenzy. More of them descended in mass to the ground for the dead man. Julian never saw vulture birds as aggressive as these in his entire life, and so many. It was as if they were materializing from thin air to swarm their victim.

But these hellish birds seemed to have developed appetites for more than just the dead. Their beaks were picking and ripping at the corpse's flesh, but their eyes were fixed on him. Julian felt that if he didn't get away immediately with Caleb Williams, the birds would drag him away, too.

Bounty Hunters

"I am the man who rode with the devil."

Julian arrived in town and it was nothing less than a madhouse. Most people hadn't gotten the news and feared being massacred by the alleged Indian war party. The two men and woman watched him approach them from their perch, a bench outside the general store. He looked around and down the street, where he finally saw the Marshal leaning against the wall just outside the entrance to a tavern.

"Wagon made it in fine?" Julian asked as he stopped Caleb Williams in front of them.

One of the men answered. "Yes it did. Much obliged to you and the other marshal."

"That was impressive wagon riding," Julian noted. "If I ever get chased, you're the man I'd pay good money to be my driver. What do you do for a living?"

"I'm a newsman, but I've done my fair share of horseback riding."

"Then you came to the right place today for a story."

"Let's see how my nerves are after I finish my whiskey.

The news can wait."

"Marshal, is it true the town is out of danger?" the woman asked.

"There's no warpath on the way here, and U.S. soldiers are nearby. The town will be safe."

"Thanks, marshal."

"It was nice meeting you gentlemen, ma'am."

Julian walked his horse to the waiting Marshal.

"What happened to you?" Marshal asked.

"Give me until tomorrow to be able to answer that question," Julian replied. "But the shooter won't be shooting anyone again—ever."

Marshal smirked. "I had no doubt of that when I saw you break away and circle back. His bad luck that he annoyed the one marshal on the planet who'd chase him down even if he had to ride to other side of the earth. I don't suppose you gave him a chance to surrender?"

"He wasn't interested in using his mouth for talking."

"I don't know what that means, but we can converse about it some other time. Let's find my fugitive so we can get back on the road to your uncle."

With their horses settled, the two men walked through the mostly empty streets to the sheriff's station. Everyone was elsewhere. The action was at the front of town.

Marshal pushed the door open with Julian just a step behind.

"Marshal 'Say-It-Twice,'" someone called out.

Waiting inside were five rugged men in similar cowboy hats and attire, standing around the main desk.

Marshal walked in and shook the enthusiastic man's hand, then waved to greet the other men. Julian noticed that one of the men, unlike the rest, was not too happy at the Marshal's arrival.

"This is Marshal Julian Crane," Marshal announced to the men.

"Another marshal," the man said. "I thought this Indian warpath wasn't headed into town."

"It isn't. We are on the trail up north." To Julian he said, "The boys are bounty hunters."

"We've taken in some notorious murders and other assorted fugitives," one man said. "American, British, French, Indian, we don't care. If the money is good, we'll take in anyone."

"Have you and the boys seen Frenchie?" Marshal asked.

"Him? No. Haven't seen him for a long while. What'd he do?"

"Murder."

"What's the bounty on him?"

Marshal smiled. "This one is mine, boys."

The lead bounty hunter, Voss, laughed. "Just foolin', Marshal. We'll tell you if we see him." He looked at Julian. "The Marshal and us have a good system. He doesn't interfere with our bounties, and we give him tips on his. We make good paydays and he…does his duty for the state of New York." Voss and the other bounty hunters laughed. "That amounts to a couple of coins, a cot, and…are they up to two hot meals a day now, Marshal?" Voss laughed louder.

"Voss, I'm glad I'm here to amuse you and the boys," Marshal said dryly.

Julian again couldn't help noticing that one of the bounty hunters seemed to want to be anywhere else but in the room. He realized that he never did ask Hans Van

Ripper why he had the same reaction to the Marshal and now wished he did.

The men spent the next twenty minutes sharing small talk until the town's sheriff finally returned. He was an elderly man, but still fit and brawny.

"Sheriff," Marshal greeted.

"Marshal. Back so soon."

"I wanted to make sure you knew we were poking around in town."

"What does he look like, and what did he do?" Sheriff Tanner asked.

Marshal fully described the man to him. Julian for the first time knew the details himself.

"Thanks for the professional courtesy," the Sheriff said. "However, if you find this man, tell me first before you try to apprehend him. I make it a point to be there when anyone is arrested in my town."

"Yes, Sheriff," Marshal responded. "Perhaps we'll stop by before you close up for the night. If not, see you in the morning."

Marshal led Julian back outside.

"We'll split up. Cover more ground faster."

"Are you sure he's here?" Julian asked.

"He's here."

Julian wondered to himself how the Marshal could be so certain. He felt it in his gut. A feeling Julian couldn't deny he had experienced a few times—something was not right.

"I knew we should never have come to New York. I hate this state. We should never have come here!" a woman yelled.

"Shut up, woman! Stop nagging me! You don't think I know? Do you think I'm going to stand and let harm come to my family?"

The couple stood at the busiest street corner of the town. Everywhere they could see the panic, and it was equally reflected in their faces.

"If we can't get away...the Indians scalp men, women, and children." She was on the verge of tears.

"Sir, I have to get out of this town immediately. My wife and children, and me."

The same man was now at a group of wagons readying to leave town.

"Sir, we have no more room on our wagon train. I'm sorry. We are taking everyone we can possibly take," the lead man said to him.

"But what am I to do? There are no horses for sale, and no other wagons to take us out of here. We must get on your wagon train."

"Sorry, sir, but we have no more room."

The man reached into his jacket to draw a gun. He aimed it at the head of the wagon train leader, who didn't blink as he stood his ground.

"We must get on your wagon train."

"What do you think you are doing?" The Marshal stood behind the man.

The man turned to look back, his face sweaty and his shaky hand holding a gun.

"I am Marshal Damian. Put that gun away now or I'll shoot *you*."

The man swallowed hard and slowly lowered his arm.

"We must escape from here, marshal," the man said. "I

can't let them kill my family."

"No one's killing your family or anyone else's. What put that notion in your head?"

"The Indian warpath—"

"There's no Indian warpath coming, at least none after Whites. Is that what everyone is still saying? Didn't you hear? One tribe was attacked by another, but they are being escorted to Fort Clinton for safety, and the Army is out in force throughout this entire region handling the situation. Those are the facts. Stop all this chaos in the streets and go about your business. You and your family can stay here in town, and you don't have anything at all to worry about."

The marshal was more directing his comments at the wagon train crowd than the man.

"No warpath?" the wagon train leader asked.

"No warpath."

The wagon train leader walked up to the man and punched him in his face, knocking him to the ground.

"I have a mind to shoot you dead for pointing a gun at me."

The Marshal stepped forward. "Sir, you got your punch in. Move on now."

The wagon leader glanced at the man on the ground and walked away.

The Marshal bent down, extended his hand to the sad man on the ground and helped him to his feet. The man's face was near tears, not from the punch he received but for his desperate behavior.

"I'm sorry I lost my head," the man said.

Marshal put a hand on the man's shoulder. "The wrong man should never lose his head." He removed his hand.

"There's not a man alive who can't relate to the emotions going through your mind."

The Marshal dusted the man's clothes off a bit.

"Where's your family?"

"They're waiting for me at the hotel."

"Go to them and enjoy the town's hospitality. There's no need for any panic. Everything is fine. I'm here," he pointed to a waiting Julian, "other lawmen are here, the Army is in the region. No warpath is going to take you from your family."

"Yes, I hear you."

"Good. Go to your family and don't point that gun at anyone like that again. I wouldn't want you to do something to make the law have to deprive your family of your person."

"Yes, marshal."

"Go to them now."

"Thank you for your kindness, marshal. Bless you, sir."

The Marshal rode off to the east part of town, and Julian covered the western part. With the news about the Indian war party spreading, people were starting to return, no longer fearful. He waited on the porch of another tavern and watched, business owners, travelers, people on foot, people on horseback, men, women and boisterous children—all returning to town to resume their routines.

His eye somehow picked out one of bounty hunters in the crowd—the one who didn't seem to like the Marshal at all. The man walked into the shop of the local gunsmith.

Julian waited patiently outside, and in a few moments, the man re-emerged and immediately stopped.

"Can I speak with you for a moment, mister?" Julian

asked.

"Why? I have nothing to say."

"I had a question or two about the Marshal."

The bounty hunter had a look of nervousness. "Get off the street."

He led Julian away, into a small alleyway to the back of the stores.

"What do you want Marshal Crane? I have nothing to say."

"Your friends were happy to see the Marshal."

"They're not my friends. They're my business partners. There's a difference."

"They were happy to see the Marshall. You weren't. Why is that?"

"Marshal Crane, if you're asking me, a total stranger, then you already know."

"Know? Mister, I've only been with the Marshal for a couple of days. I've never met him before in my life. You know him better than I do. Is there something you know about the Marshal that I should? I am traveling north with him alone."

"That's unfortunate for you. The Marshal is evil."

Julian stared at the bounty hunter. It was not the response he had expected. "Please, explain what that means?"

"Why are you riding with him?"

"He's taking me to a man I thought was dead."

"And the Marshal is the only one who's seen him alive?"

"Yes."

The bounty hunter shook his head. "Did you think this man was dead before? Others thought he was dead?"

"Yes. So?"

"Then the man is dead, Marshal."

"How could you say—?"

"Marshal, I don't care how you do it, but get away from him as quickly as you can. He's tricking you, and wherever he's taking you, don't go. You go and you probably won't come back. That's all I have to say. I have to go."

Julian grabbed him by the shoulder. "Mister, you can't make that kind of allegation to me and then walk away. I'm a lawman myself."

"I thought lawmen had the uncanny ability to size a man up? If you stopped me, then you already know something is wrong."

"I don't know anything. I simply noticed your expression when you first saw him at the sheriff's. That's why I'm asking what you know."

"Didn't you ask about his background?"

"Of course, yes. Before becoming a lawman, he was a simple farmer," the bounty hunter let out a laugh, "before he joined the War."

"He was never no farmer. He was a bounty hunter. He was all over the Thirteen Colonies hunting for scalp money. He looked much different back then. No one would recognize him. I do only because I saw him over the years as he changed, and my appearance changed too. Back then he was a big man, fat, not lanky as he is today, and his hair color was fair."

"What do you mean scalp money?"

"You know what I mean, marshal. There was big bounty money to be had back then. Some group of settlers or another wanting to *clear* their land of Indians, sometimes even a settler or two they didn't like. He even got other Indians to pay him bounties in goods to go after other Indian tribes they were at war with. He'd kill, scalp, skin, burn anyone—English, French, colonist, Indian, African. Behead people even."

Julian felt sick to his stomach as he stared at the man.

"Surely, as a lawman yourself, you knew all the not-so-nice things that went on before the War and during the War, too, on all sides. Or are you one of those people who believe such horrors don't happen on God's green earth?"

"I fought in the War myself, so I surely don't belief that. I've seen the cruelty of men with my own eyes. I once saw a woman hack a mob to pieces. And I have seen the victims of scalping attacks, both White and Indian. I know this country's history, all of it, and it's nothing different than any other country. I just never understood the need for the scalp."

"How else would you give proof of death to get your bounty? Drag the whole body back? Carry around a bag full of heads? Scalps were the most logical thing to do. It was about quantity back then. For the money."

"To think we taught and encouraged such a thing among the Indians."

"They didn't need to be taught and encouraged to do anything, marshal. They knew all about savagery long before Whites arrived on this land, the bad ones. Ask my wife. She's Indian, and she's a better history teacher than any White man will ever be. I have to go, marshal."

The bounty hunter tried to walk away again, but Julian stopped him.

"Please, mister. I can't believe what you're saying about the Marshal. He's a longtime lawman...well, at least for the past seven or ten years."

"So?" the man interjected. "The law attracts men both good and bad. You know that better than I do."

"But how do you know all this? You said you recognized him over the years."

"How do you think, marshal? I had a family to feed. But I never did any of the things he did, what many of them did. I have to go marshal."

"Shouldn't you say something, do something about the Marshal?"

"No one will believe us. He has friends all over this region. Only a few people living know who he is. He's two people, the Marshal. The one everyone sees and likes, and the other him, the evil one. That's the side he hides from everyone."

"Then you must tell what you know."

"I gotta go. And another thing. I don't believe for a second that Frenchie murdered anybody. The Marshal probably did it and Frenchie saw him do it, whatever it is."

"Mister, you have a duty to go to sheriff with this then."

The bounty hunter laughed. "Bye, Marshal Crane." The man pushed past him and disappeared around the corner.

Julian felt a wave of panic. He ran to his horse.

He found what he was looking for—the Marshal's horse tied to a livery stable. Julian jumped down from Caleb Williams and ran. He stopped everyone he could to find out if they had seen the Marshal. One man knew him and pointed.

Julian could hear voices in a heated conversation

behind the church. Julian slowly peered around the corner and saw the two men. It was the Marshal and another man who was short and round.

"Why are you lying on me!" the man said in a French accent. "I'm going to tell everyone about you!"

The Marshal drew and shot the man in the chest!

Wagon Train

"How do you kill a devil of a thing?"

Frenchie's lifeless body hung over the rear of the horse as the Marshal rode to the Sheriff's station. The Sheriff and a deputy happened to be outside when they saw him coming.

The Marshal dismounted as Julian rode up on Caleb Williams.

"Sorry, Sheriff. I couldn't bring him in alive," Marshal said. "He was a raving maniac. Pointed his gun right at my head and told me that he wasn't going to go back to face the law unless he was dead. I gave him what he wanted."

The town sheriff walked over to the body and lifted up Frenchie's head.

The Sheriff looked at Julian. "Where were you in all this?"

"I was on the other side of town, sheriff," Julian answered. "I was coming back to check in. Glad I did. I would have been searching for this Frenchie for hours for nothing."

"And you show up at the exact moment your friend meanders on back with his fugitive?"

"I heard the shot, Sheriff."

The Sheriff seemed satisfied.

"Am I able to process this so we can be off on our way?" the Marshal asked.

The Sheriff looked at the dead man again on the horse and nodded. "Yes, I'll attest to it as a righteous shooting."

"Thanks Sheriff."

Marshal and Julian took the body to the town's undertaker and then galloped back to the Sheriff's. The five bounty hunters were going in the opposite direction heading out of town.

"Until next time, Marshal," the lead bounty hunter said with a smile.

"See you boys." Marshal waved good-bye.

Julian's eyes locked on the fifth bounty hunter for a brief moment. He didn't look back. The bounty hunters rode off.

"Don't play with danger." His father always said to him. Julian and his friends were reckless little boys. He now thought to himself how much like Brom Bones and his Sleepy Hollow Boys he and his friends must have been. They all probably would have been part of the same gang had they lived in the same town.

When he was a kid, there was a vicious dog in town, and Julian was determined to be the terror of the animal. As he waited near their neighbor's house, he could smell the beautiful aroma inside from his hiding place. The neighbor's wife always baked pies at the beginning of the week. He crept in and snatched a full pie right from the kitchen table when the mother left to attend to her new baby.

He had it all planned and could barely stifle his own giggling. He'd find that vicious dog, sneak up to it, and hurl the pie at its face. It would be stunned and run off yelping down the street. He'd be the hero of the town, and all his mates would brag about what he did for weeks.

When little Julian launched the pie from his hand into the dog's face, he did not expect what happened. It did not jump or run away yelping. It glared at him with a meanness that scared Julian to his toes. The dog attacked him and proceeded to maul him until passersby kicked the dog senseless to get it to finally stop attacking. The only story that went through town was how the vicious dog, foaming at the mouth so profusely, nearly devoured young Julian. He never told anyone that the foaming was the filling from a pie he'd stolen. Though the neighbor's wife kept the front door locked after that day.

His father always knew the truth somehow. His mother cried over him but his father only stared at him. "You keep playing with danger and someone will end up dead. Your mother won't be able to kiss your cheek and make it all better." He did listen, for a time. His adolescence brought the recklessness back, and it would take another event so horrific that it still came to him in nightmares to make him stop for good. But now there was this.

Later, there was the sight of the undertaker riding up the street with the cheap, pine box with Frenchie's body inside headed for the cemetery. Unlike the amiable Mr. Berg in Sleepy Hollow, this town's undertaker looked like a living ghoul. Most of the teeth were gone from his mouth and, as skinny as his uncle Ichabod was, this man's body was skeletal. He touched his black hat as he passed in his dusty black clothes.

The Marshal killed a man in cold blood. He saw it with his own eyes. He was "two men" as that bounty hunter had said. Why not run? Run now, just as the bounty hunter told him to do, but Julian refused. He had to know what the Marshal had planned. He had to know where he was leading him and why. He had to verify what his gut was already telling his head about his uncle and the "good" Marshal. He had to play with danger again, this time.

He told many, many people to always listen to their gut, and especially if their head was telling them something different. When it came to danger, your gut feeling was always superior to your intellect. Humans were animals, and that gut feeling is what kept the species alive. Intellect was the pompousness that grew over the centuries from humans believing they were too good for those innate animal instincts that served them so well over the ages. If you turn to walk down a dark alley and your gut tells you not to, then don't. If you're riding alone down a deserted path and your gut tells you that someone is watching you, then you are being watched. If you're gut tells you that Marshal is going to kill you the first chance he gets…

"My little detour is done," Marshal said to him. "We'll finish up with the Sheriff and go."

"Will we not stay in town the night?"

"I don't see why we need to. It'll take us a few days to get there and we have some good hours of light before we have stop to set up camp. We stay and who knows what other people or causes will come up to delay us again."

Julian smiled. "Since we'll be in the open for a few days, let's stay the night in town. I'll take a hotel bed over the cold ground any day, even if it's only one night. We can leave at dawn."

"Yes, Marshal Crane."

The sun peeked across the horizon as the men rode out as planned. Marshal took the lead and Julian stayed close. He eyed the Marshal's horse and thought to himself—Body Snatcher. He remembered thinking to himself at the time that it was a peculiar name for a horse. Maybe it had even more of a meaning than he knew. Julian started to recall everything the Marshal had said from their first meeting.

Anyone else would probably have run away from the Marshal as soon as they could. The Marshal was probably thinking Julian was "stuck" with him for the trip to Ichabod, but that wasn't it at all. If Ichabod was truly alive, he didn't need the Marshal or anyone else to find him. Julian wanted to play this cat-and-mouse game to the end.

But the question did enter his head. *Who was the cat? Who was the mouse?*

They came across a large wagon train that was also heading north and were welcomed in to join them. It was made up of about thirty families with children and about forty or so men. Their redheaded leader was happy to have not one but two marshals to accompany them.

Marshal and Julian rode next to their leader at the front. His horse looked much like Caleb Williams, but the man's saddle was ornate for a simple shopkeeper.

"The saddle has been in my family for so many years that we forgot who its first owner was and the history around it. I will pass it down to my son and he to his. That's how we do things. We keep 'em to last.

"How long have you been lawmen?" Red asked them.

"Seven years," Marshal answered.

"Just over a year for me," Julian said. "But both of us are ex-soldiers too, from the War."

"We are so happy you marshals came upon us." Red smiled. "God must be looking down upon us."

"What's that around your neck?" Julian asked.

"Oh, my silly rabbit's foot charm," he answered. "A gift from my late mother. I wear it for her, but it has given me good luck over the years."

"How long have you been on the trail?" Marshal asked.

"Three weeks. We're almost to our destination, just south of the Canadian border. We're going to make a new life for ourselves."

"It gets cold up there," Julian said.

"We are stout folks. When a man has a home to call his own, no weather is too harsh, no matter where it is."

"You and your people sound like the kind of folk I'd expect to head out west," Julian added.

"Well, we are not that brave, at least not yet. Maybe one day we will."

The climate had already started to get chillier, but with the nearing of the end of October and moving north towards the Canadian border, there would be some mornings and nights that would be downright frigid—a small taste of the coming winter.

"What's it like to be a lawman?" the son asked. The boy was seventeen years old, and the eldest of Red's children.

"It's a good feeling," Julian answered. "Keeping the peace."

The Marshal stifled a smile. Julian felt no need to share with the young man his recent hypocritical actions.

"You're protecting the people but it's more than that," the son continued. "You are the good fighting the forces of evil. That's what you do. How do you marshals feel about that?"

"I never thought of it that way, but…yes you have it right. But I would say all of us do our part to fight the bad in our own small way or in big ways when needed. It doesn't matter."

"How do you feel about it, Marshal?" the son asked.

Marshal looked at him a moment and his gaze moved down to the ground. "I'm not sure. I'll think on it and let you know my answer."

"Oh don't mind him, Marshal," Red interjected. "My son should be a philosopher. The only problem is no one will pay you a living to be one."

Julian said to the son, "There's nothing wrong with a good hobby to occupy your time."

The son nodded.

"Do you expect any trouble on the trip, Marshal?" Red asked.

"None at all," Marshal responded. "Your wagon train should reach Middletown on schedule without incident."

"When do you have to turn off?"

"We'll be able to stay with you until sometime tomorrow, but you'll be fine without us."

"I wish you could see us 'til the end. I know it would make everyone feel easier."

"You'll be fine."

"I'll tell the women to try to coax you to stay with some of our downright, heavenly home cookin' away from home."

The men laughed. "We like that kind of coaxing,"

Julian added.

The trek was as smooth as could be. The wagons stopped midday along the river for the lunch meal, and rest and water for the horses. The marshals learned that the group was originally from the Carolinas but wanted to find wide-open space to form their own town. The allure of the "new" was still a powerful feeling among a lot of people. Many were content being settled in an established town, but there were plenty who were adventurers at heart. It was a feeling Julian himself could relate to. Most of America remained uncharted land.

When time came to make their final stop for the night, the wagons were arranged in a circle, a few men were posted at the perimeter to guard, and people settled in around the roaring fire made in the center of camp. Most relaxed by the campfire, eating supper and would pass the time with a good ghost story for at least a couple of hours.

Julian sat on the ground comfortably with one knee propped up and his forearm and chin resting upon it. Marshal was lying flat on the ground with the rim of his hat covering his eyes and nose. He had no interest in ghost stories.

A man was serious in his recounting to the group. "I've met many a hunter, especially those who've been closer to the far northern colonies, I mean states, and Canada who have seen it."

"What was it?" one of the smaller children asked.

"No one knows. They first thought it was a giant bear of some kind. We've only explored the eastern seaboard of this continent, and so much of it is unknown, especially moving west. There could be countless species of animals we haven't encountered yet. This beast must be at least twice the height of a normal man, but it's not a bear. It's man-like."

"How they know how tall it is?" the same boy asked.

"The size of its feet," the man answered. "And it naturally walks on two feet. Bears will walk on all fours most of the time and leap up on two legs only when they want to get something up high or terrify its prey."

"Big feet, huh?"

"Yep."

"There're all kinds of legends about people turning into animals and animals turning into people. Maybe it's one of them. It could be a whole tribe of them and they change to get away. I learned about it from the Indians. There's even have a fancy word for it. 'Trans-morg' or something such like. The people trans-morg into animals or animals trans-morg into people."

"Witches have done that for centuries. That's why you have to burn them," one of the women said.

"It's called transmogrification," another man butted in.

The storyteller began again. "Yep, that's it. Just because we have all our book-knowledge and conveniences in these modern times, we mustn't forget that there is still the supernatural. I've seen it."

"Oh, what about the sea monster Rip saw last year?" a man called out. The statement got a whole round of acknowledgment from the camp.

"Did they find it again?"

"No, they searched that whole river right out to the Atlantic."

"Tell me what it looked like," the boy asked.

"It was some kind of giant sea serpent encased in a shiny slime."

"The water is the most dangerous place. You can never see what's lurking beneath the surface," a woman said. "You will never see me or my children swimming in any river or lake."

"I was by Pennsylvania, and they told me about the Dark Trapper that prowls those parts," one man said. "We just found out about it, but the Indians have known about him for centuries."

"Centuries?" the boy asked.

"It's the size of a man, covered in fur skins, including its fur cap. It has fox feet, clawed hands, and no face."

"No face?" the boy asked. "Then how does it eat?" People laughed.

"How am I supposed to know? All I know is it hunts men. A man thinks he tracking a fox or coyote and it's the Dark Trapper. It kills the men and scatters their remains throughout the forest."

"It has to do that because it has no mouth to eat," a woman blurted out. People began to laugh again.

"Tell me about this Headless Horseman I heard about around a place called Sleepy Hollow," Julian called out. "How do you kill it?"

Everyone turned to look at him.

"You can't kill a ghost, sonny," an old man answered.

"Every ghost or goblin can be defeated," Julian said. "Maybe you don't know the one I mean."

"Oh, we do," the old man countered. "The Legendary Headless Horseman. The Galloping Hessian of Sleepy Hollow. Had his head blown clean off by a cannon ball in the War, and now he haunts the region in search of it and carries off any unfortunate victims who come across his path. Haunts the region by night, and must return to the town's church graveyard before sunrise."

"You can't kill it, but you can drive it off for a short time," another man said. "You have to stay beyond the reach of its power. It can't cross water so you cross a bridge and your safe, but…"

"But what?" Julian asked.

"It can throw its horrible missile—that devilish pumpkin—at you no matter how far you run. It can get you that way."

"Sonny, the key to defeating it is its lair. The land it dwells in and where it rests when the sun rises until night comes for it to ride again. Destroy that place and you destroy it," the original storytelling man said.

Other people in the camp agreed, and Julian sat quietly in deep thought.

The man continued with his ghost stories to occupy the camp until it was time to sleep.

Julian happened throw a glance over at Marshal. He was no longer lying flat but sitting upright, glaring at the storytelling man. The fire glistened in the Marshal's eyes. He was boiling with rage.

About Marshal

"Julian Crane is done dead?"

Both men thought to themselves that they would never want to be out in the open in this land at night or during any inclement weather. The wind seemed chillier, shadows seemed to take on a life of their own, and darkened forests were especially to be avoided. The trees always looked like they would jump up and run after you at any moment. A day ago, they could have sworn that two crows they saw had been talking to each other, but immediately stopped when they realized the men were there. This was one creepy place, and neither man could think of any other that was more so.

Two days before, they came across a man originally from a nearby town that said he had been hunting a deer when it double-backed at him and tried to bite him with what he swore were fangs. Of course, the account elicited loud laughter from the men crowding the local tavern, until he said he had been near the town of Sleepy Hollow and then proceeded to lift up his shirt and show them all the visible bite marks into his side.

The Headless Horseman was supposedly gone. However, did the Horseman make the land haunted, or did the haunted land attract the Horseman to begin with? But then again, all of it could have all been figments of their minds after years of hearing any number of ghost stories about these parts, and who knew how much of it was from pranksters.

"So this is Sleepy Hollow, the place with all those stories of the Headless Horseman?" the younger man asked.

"Yep," the older man on point answered. "The Legend of Sleepy Hollow."

The two riders moved at a relaxed pace, as if they didn't have a care in the world. Their horses were old but still reliable. Their clothes were older but kept them as comfortable as needed for the weeklong trip to the Tappan Zee area.

The younger man asked, "Have you heard of any stories recently from there?"

"No, but that doesn't mean there aren't any. Towns are like their own world. All kinds of things can happen and no one living in another world will know anything about it."

"But we used to hear about them all the time. I remember. But nothing for a long while."

"Yep, several years back there were lots of jabbering about them and their Headless Horseman. But people get bored and look for the next story."

"What happened to this Headless Horseman's head?"

"He was supposed to be some kind of Hessian soldier whose head was taken clean off by cannon fire. The story goes that he patrolled nightly for it, and went after the lone, unsuspecting traveler, too. Probably to get theirs instead."

"That's one way to keep people off your roads at night." The younger man laughed.

"We're not here to fool around." The older man got more serious.

"I know." The younger man decided to change the subject back to what they had spent most of their days planning. "Do you think we'll catch up to him?"

"Maybe."

"Do you think he's the one behind it?"

"We don't know if there is even a crime yet."

"We know there is. We don't know how bad yet, that's all."

Old-timer Mr. Berg stood on the corner of the main street into town, his hands holding the lapels of his coat. He watched the two riders draw nearer with his pipe hanging from his lips like always. He had noticed the men when they were about a half-mile out.

Only now had Tarry Town gotten back to normal after the whole "Julian Affair," but people's nerves were still fragile. Town leaders had put out the word to look out for any other out-of-place strangers coming into town. They were not about to allow any other visitors smooth-talk their way into homes or the town again. No one expected to see Julian Crane again, but they especially wanted to make sure he didn't come back to start a whole new bit of chaos.

"Hello, sir." The older man of the two riders had a big bushy mustache.

"Hello," Berg casually answered.

The younger man looked like he could be the older one's son.

"Do you have a town lawman I could speak to?" the older man asked.

"Can't say we're big enough for all that, but soon. Why do you need a lawman? Are you reporting something or turning yourself in before someone has to report you?"

The older man laughed and the younger one smiled.

"Funny. No, we're doing some investigating of some potential crimes."

"Are you lawmen?"

"We are in a way."

"Marshals?"

"No, I was a lawman a long time ago. My son here plans to be. Let's just say I'm helping out a sheriff friend of ours. If I could speak to a person in authority, I would explain everything in full."

"Seems that you two are quite a ways from any kind of jurisdiction."

"We're citizens, not lawmen. We're just helping a lawman."

"Hmm." Berg stood there thinking.

"What work do you do in town?"

"I'm the undertaker. I take you under when its time."

The two men laughed again.

"Then we don't want to know you," the older man said.

"What are you investigating exactly? You said potential crimes."

"Yes, but I'd like to talk to someone in authority first. I know if it were my town, I wouldn't like it a bit if strangers were poking around."

Berg nodded. "I appreciate that consideration."

"You're welcome."

Berg was now more open to helping them, but he had to be sure. "But why here, mister?"

"Not here. We're passing though to get to Sleepy Hollow."

Berg was suspicious again.

"Why would you need to go to Sleepy Hollow?"

"That is the adjacent town? We were told it was only about two miles away."

"It is, but why go there? Tarry Town is the main town. Sleepy Hollow is where our locals live. Visitors have no cause to be there unless invited."

"We're looking for someone."

Berg thought to himself, *I knew it. That Julian Crane had caused trouble in other places too and people are out looking for him.*

"Is that someone you're looking for called Julian Crane?"

The older man answered back, "No. Who's that?"

The local church had a small community room for ad-hoc meetings, and the two men felt more comfortable discussing their business. Berg arrived with two town elders, Koning and Boer, who wanted to find out what the two strangers wanted before going further.

"Morning gentleman, my name's Allan and this is my eldest son Allen junior," the man said as he shook their hands. "Thanks for interrupting your day to see me."

"What can we do for you, sir?" Koning asked.

"Do you know a man named Damian Marshal?"

"I do. He's the marshal for our region."

The man glanced at his son for a moment.

"Why?" Koning asked. "Is there a problem?"

"I'm going to ask one question, and it's important you answer it truthfully so I know how to proceed with my words. My intent is not to ruffle anyone's feathers, but you'll soon learn why we came all this way. Have any of you noticed anything strange about your marshal?"

The Elders looked at each, confused.

"That's a thing to ask," Boer said. "Strange about the marshal? No, not at all."

"Mr. Berg said you didn't know a Julian Crane, but this is precisely the type of outrageous things he was saying when he came to town."

"About the marshal?"

"No. About other upstanding citizen of our community."

"Oh, well as I said before we don't know a Julian Crane, and I don't care to know him."

"Pa," the younger man said to get the older man's attention.

He looked at his son and saw him pointing to Berg. They looked to him.

"What about you, sir?" Allen asked.

The Elders looked at him, too, and it was clear to all of them that he knew something.

"Don't get excited," Berg said. "Not me, but Hans has always had bad feelings towards him and...."

"And what?" Koning asked.

"So does Mr. Van Brunt."

The Elders were surprised.

"Mr. Van Brunt, too?"

Berg nodded.

"We were told that the people of Sleepy Hollow would be able to tell us everything about this marshal, and it seems that it's true. Can we speak with these two men?"

"First, you tell us what this is about."

"Sir, my son and I are from down south in Tennessee. Our lawman couldn't make the trip so he sent us instead. We know for certain that one man who was with this marshal of yours disappeared and has never been seen again, and we have reason to believe that one or more other men may have also fallen to foul play at the hands of this marshal. We have no proof, but we need to speak with him just the same."

"You think he has something to do with three disappearances?"

"Yes, we do."

"Why are you so certain about one of the men?"

"Because I was there. The man is my best friend and my son's godfather. He was distressed over losing touch with his eldest daughter, and this marshal showed up and said he knew exactly where she was and he'd personally take him to her. Three months after they left, we all found out that the daughter had died giving birth to her first child and her husband died from fever, which is why he couldn't reach them. All this happened five years ago. The marshal never did see them as he claimed, so where did he take my son's godfather, and why hasn't he ever come back?"

The look on the faces of the three men made Allen stop talking, and made his son stand from his chair.

"What did I say?" Allen asked.

One of the town elders turned to the others. "I think we better get Mr. De Graaf."

De Graaf stood at the main desk opposite the innkeeper.

"Did you notice anything?"

"Notice anything, Mr. De Graaf? No. They just rode out of town side-by-side. What should I have noticed?"

"Never mind." De Graaf turned. Now it wasn't just the two strangers, Berg and two elders. The lobby had filled up with other businesspeople.

"Please, everyone go about your business."

"What's happening, Mr. De Graaf? Is there more trouble coming into town?" a man asked.

"No, nothing." He gestured for the two strangers to follow him outside.

"Can we come, Mr. De Graaf?" Berg asked.

"I'd prefer not," he answered.

"But my wagon is already hitched up. I can take you out to Van Ripper's place right away."

De Graaf considered his offer. "Okay, wait out back, and we'll come out after I'm done speaking with these two gentlemen."

Berg smiled and walked out the main door ahead of them.

De Graaf hurried the other two men along outside and then across the street to his barrister office. It was a small one-room building but well maintained and suitable for his purposes. He unlocked the door and once the men were in, closed it. Through the windows, he could already see people on the streets watching them.

"Gentlemen, have a seat anywhere."

"We can stand."

"Yes, but I think I will sit."

De Graaf walked to his main desk and collapsed in the

large chair.

"Is everything you told us so far the truth?" he asked bluntly.

"It is, sir," Allen answered.

"In your mind, what do you think happened to your friend? You can tell me."

"I believe your marshal killed him and the other two men that we know of."

De Graaf was sickened by the implications. "My God, the man's been in my home more times than I can count. Why would he do that? He's been a marshal in these parts for over six years, no, seven years. Why? What motive could he possibly have?"

"My job is just to find him, sir. Motive for murder is not my business."

"Are you authorized to apprehend a U.S. Marshal?"

"I am not, but my son and I will defend ourselves, and we would like to have that authority to hold him, or have the town designate an authority to hold him until another marshal arrives, or until we can send for my sheriff."

"You live in these parts and every day is nice and quiet and then all of this happens," De Graaf said aloud to himself. "You'll have the town's authority to hold him if only to allow him the opportunity to clear his name, but...I must accompany you on your investigation every step of the way. We had another party here before acting on his own, and it led to eight men being beaten nearly to death and strung from a tree. We barely averted an all-out shoot-out in our streets. I can't stand gunplay."

"That's why we sought you out, sir. We'll abide by the town's wishes."

"I appreciate how you have conducted yourselves in

our town. I wish more people were as courteous. We'll go out to Hans Van Ripper's place first and then out to Mr. Van Brunt."

"That's satisfactory to us," Allen said.

"May we ask a question?" Allen Junior asked.

"Yes, certainly."

"Why did everyone behave so strangely when we told them the circumstances of your marshal when we last saw my godfather?"

"Because it is exactly the circumstances that occurred a few days ago, only instead of your godfather, it was a man named Julian Crane."

"It doesn't sound like he's too popular here," Allen said.

"He isn't, but he doesn't deserve to be murdered."

"If the circumstances are similar, who was the person the marshal said he saw but was dead?" Allen asked.

"Julian Crane's uncle, Ichabod Crane, our local schoolmaster. Ten years ago."

"Who killed his uncle?" Allen junior asked.

De Graaf stood from his chair. "I think we should get to Hans Van Ripper's place right away."

Hans Van Ripper stood outside his cabin chopping wood. This time he was doing it not just for something to do but also for when it got colder. His body would not budge out of bed to go anywhere near outside then, so he needed a big supply of firewood. When the chill was in the air, it was not unusual for him to keep the fireplace going all day and all night long.

He heard the noises on the hill and looked up to see a group of riders. He immediately noticed De Graaf from his stove top hat, but he had never seen the two men with him before.

"Hello Hans," De Graaf called out.

Van Ripper stopped and waited for the men to get closer. The two men looked to be father and son.

"Hello," Van Ripper said with an annoyed voice. "Who's with you?"

"This is Mister Allen senior and Allen junior," De Graaf answered. "Up from the Tennessee area. Can we talk inside for a moment? It's important."

Hans turned and carried his ax through the door. The men followed him into the cabin. Hans leaned the ax in the corner.

"I don't have much to eat in here, and I can't offer much in the way of drink either."

"That's not necessary, Hans. We don't have time for that," De Graaf said impatiently.

"Thanks anyway, sir," the older man said.

Hans was able to appreciate the man's manners even if he had none to reciprocate.

"You all can have a seat," he said to them.

De Graaf led the two men to a couple of chairs and he sat on the desk. Hans grabbed a small stool.

"What's so important?" Hans asked.

"Hans, we were told in town that you have some kind of issue with the Marshal."

"Who said that?"

"Hans, please tell us what the issue is you have with the Marshal?" De Graaf asked. "Why don't you care for him?"

"I have no issue with the Marshal, and there's no law that says I have to like everyone."

The three other men looked at one another and realized

that Hans was not going to be forthcoming.

"Maybe I should explain," Allen senior said.

As he recounted his story as he done for Berg, the elders, and De Graaf before, Hans' face changed from indifference to concern and then to fear.

"You don't need to tell me anymore." He looked at De Graaf and asked, "What do you intend to do? Julian Crane is out with him now."

"There's not much we can do. We don't know where exactly they headed so it would be impossible to trace them."

Hans stood up from his chair and paced the floor. "We better not lose another Crane in this world."

"Hans, tell us what you know about the Marshal." De Graaf asked again.

"I don't know anything. One day, years ago, I think he was only the marshal for a year or two, I came up on him in my wagon, and he was along the side of the road burying something."

The men perked up.

"What was it?" De Graaf asked.

"Bloody clothes."

"Whose?" De Graaf asked.

"I don't know that. How would I know that?"

"Why didn't you tell someone?"

"Tell someone what? I came back later and nothing was there. I knew if I had said anything he would deny it or have some excuse about it, and I had no proof. Everyone loved our good marshal, but after that, I never trusted him, never allowed myself to be alone with him, and never let him in my house without other people around."

The younger Allen shook his head. "You all had

suspicions and did nothing?"

Hans stopped pacing and looked at him. "Do what? Everybody acts suspiciously at one time or another. Lord knows I do, but it don't mean a thing. If it were more or other people too, but it was just me. Nobody was going to listen to me and take my suspicions over a lawman that had people singing his praises from up and down the Hudson. Nobody."

"There is one other person," De Graaf revealed.

"Who?"

"Mr. Van Brunt."

Hans was shocked. "Brom Bones? What happened between Brom Bones and the Marshal? I never heard that. How do you know?"

"Berg told us, but we don't know the particulars."

"I never heard that before. I wonder for how long? I wonder if anyone else knows something."

"If there is anyone else, by now they'll be coming forward. The word is probably everywhere by now, here and in town."

"Sir, I hope none of your people try to be heroes," the older Allen added.

"Oh, no, Mr. Allen. The Marshal shows up and the whole town will find us." He turned to Van Ripper again. "Hans, is there anything else? Anything else he did or said?"

"No. But I think he knew I was always watching him so he was extra careful."

"Do you have any questions?" De Graaf asked the Allens.

"No, that's it. We can go to this Van Brunt now."

"I'm coming, too," Hans announced.

"You don't need to, Hans." De Graaf stood up from the desk.

"I'm coming. I want to know what we're going to do about this."

"We only have suspicions," De Graaf said.

"I'm coming too and that's final."

Diedrich Knickerbocker arrived at the Van Brunt estate early in the morning. He came in on a rather small horse for the man. As requested, Jansen took him to see Dutch and his men who were all back to work despite their still visually bruised and cut faces, in addition to their other healing wounds.

"What do you want to see us for?" Dutch asked.

"I wanted to see how you were all recovering."

"We're recovering."

"Good. That's all. I'm here to see your boss."

"Why?"

"It's nothing. I won't be here long at all. Just a few words and I'll be gone again."

Diedrich attempted to smile and turned to leave the man alone.

"Knickerbocker," Dutch called out.

He turned around. "Yes?"

"Thanks for checking in on us."

Diedrich had a genuine smile on his face. "You're welcome, Mr. Dutch."

Mr. Jansen and Ms. De Paul escorted Knickerbocker to the sitting room where both Brom Bones and Old Man Van Tassel were standing, waiting. Van Tassel had a "favorite" pipe and Brom was smoking a cigar.

Suddenly a door burst open and young Peter ran in. He

looked at Knickerbocker with a toy rifle in his arms.

"Hi, Mr. Knickerbocker."

"Good morning, Peter. What's that in your hands?"

"It's my rifle. I take it with me everywhere now so if that bad man comes 'round again to hurt my father, I'll get 'em."

"Your father is lucky to have a son like you to protect him."

"Peter, go and play outside," Brom said to him.

"Come on Peter." Mrs. De Paul reached out her hand as she walked to him. Peter took it and she walked him out of the room.

"How can we help you, Mr. Knickerbocker?" Katrina asked as she strolled into the room to join her husband and father.

"Oh, good. You're all here now."

Knickerbocker held his hat in his hands rather than give it to any of the servants. He nervously looked down to the ground trying to get up enough courage to talk.

"Well, you see, I wanted to wait until everything calmed down a bit. And I wanted Dutch and your other men to be up and around again."

"Diedrich, out with it," Brom directed. "What can we do for you?"

"I'm here to apologize, Mr. Van Brunt."

"Apologize?" Brom asked. "About what?"

"About Julian Crane."

The name still elicited strong negative feelings from the Van Brunts.

"What about Julian Crane?" Brom asked.

"I'm the one responsible for him getting the idea in his head that you had something to do with his uncle's death."

"You?" Katrina asked.

"Yes. I guess I opened up my mouth to the wrong people and somehow he found out about me, and he sent me a letter by post. We corresponded, and I, well, perhaps I should have been more cautious about what I wrote. I never imagined he was any kind of marshal or that he was going to come here and do what he did. I...possibly embellished my story too much, and he took it for the gospel truth. Yes, it was all my fault."

"What did you tell him exactly?" Katrina asked.

Brom was visibly nervous. "He doesn't have to get into all that. It's not important at this point. He's gone. He's going to see his uncle, supposedly, and we'll never see him again. No need for Mr. Knickerbocker to bring up the past."

His wife looked at her husband suspiciously. Brom looked back at Knickerbocker.

"Diedrich, thank you for telling us. We do appreciate it. Everyone makes mistakes. I'll forget about it, if you do."

"Oh yes, Mr. Van Brunt. I'll forget all about it right now."

"Good, then it's forgotten."

"Thanks, Mr. Van Brunt."

Knickerbocker was smiling and returned his hat to his head. Then realizing, took it off his head again.

"Jansen, you can show Diedrich to his horse," Brom said.

"Yes sir. Thanks, Mr. Van Brunt, Mrs. Van Brunt, Mr. Van Tassel."

The head butler led Knickerbocker out of the room. Brom gave a heavy sigh and turned his gaze to them. His father-in-law and wife were both watching him.

"Something you want to tell us, son?" the Old Man asked.

Brom put his cigar in his mouth and shook his head. "No."

"Are you certain?" Katrina asked.

"I'm certain I don't want to talk about something that took place before I was married and before my son was born. I'm certain."

The head butler returned to the room.

"Sir, Mr. De Graaf is here to see you. He has Hans Van Ripper and some other men with him and he'd like to speak with Knickerbocker, too."

Brom was intrigued. "Bring them in then, Jansen."

When Brom saw De Graaf's face, he put down his cigar on the tray on one of the wall desks knowing that something was wrong.

"Look at all this," Old Van Tassel said. "What has happened now? I've never seen so much goings on in such a short span of time in all the years I've lived in the Hollow."

"De Graaf what's wrong?" Brom asked.

"Is this about that Julian Crane?" Katrina asked, and Brom quickly looked at De Graaf for his answer.

"No, but it could involve him."

"I'd say it does a lot more than that," Hans said gruffly.

"Please, Hans, let me get the Van Brunts up-to-date." He looked at the Allens. "Or would you prefer to?"

"You're doing fine," the elder Allen said back.

"These two men are the Allens, father and son," De Graaf introduced. "They rode in this morning looking for the Marshal."

"What happened that you would need a marshal?" Van Tassel asked.

"No, they need to find the Marshal, personally."

The younger Allen was as impatient as Hans Van Ripper to get things moving along and jumped in. He told them briefly about his father's background and his own, living and growing up in Tennessee. He told them about his godfather overwrought about his missing daughter, and how they met Marshal Damian who came into town to tell them that he would take the man to his eldest child, having seen her to be well.

"The Marshal went all the way to that town to tell the man that he has seen his missing daughter?" Hans asked. "Rather than just send a letter. That's not his territory."

"We didn't sense anything suspicious about it at the time," the elder Allen said.

The Van Brunts had the same reaction when the young man recounted how he and his father learned that their godfather's daughter had died two years earlier, and his godfather had not been seen nor heard of since leaving with the Marshal. The Marshal was alive and well doing his duties, but he never saw fit to return to their town to explain what happened. He ended with the fact that two other men who came across the Marshal had also disappeared.

"What do you believe happened, Mr. Allen?" Katrina asked.

"I don't want to speculate, ma'am, but I do believe foul play is involved," the elder Allen answered. "We need to confront the Marshal and have him explain himself as to the whereabouts of my son's godfather. I already know he could come up with plausible explanations, but we need him to commit himself to a story and hold him while we verify it. My best friend was not a man to disappear off the earth and leave his affairs unattended to."

"Mr. Van Brunt," De Graaf began, "we've been inquiring with anyone who had any…issues with the Marshal. Hans was one, and we were told that you were the other. Is that true?"

Brom hesitated but that only firmly answered the question. He thought for a bit before he began to talk.

"Back when Ichabod Crane disappeared, before the Marshal was the marshal, he was one of the men in town helping us look for him. He had been a lawman in some town I can't remember, and he took a full account of Ichabod's dress and belongings when he left your party that night." Brom glanced at Old Man Van Tassel before he continued. "The Marshal had interviewed everyone thoroughly, and I looked it over myself and saw that he had added an item. I asked him where the account had come from, and he pulled some name out of the air that I knew was a lie. He said that Ichabod was wearing a red spotted handkerchief, but he wasn't."

"How can you be so sure, son?" Van Tassel asked.

"Because it was my handkerchief," Brom answered. "I had one of the girls at the party give it to him to wear when he rode home that night. He didn't take it out and put it on until he was well out of view of the mansion and well on his way."

"How do you know that?" Katrina asked.

"Because I saw him wearing it."

"You mean you saw him wearing it when you set on after him dressing up to look like the Headless Horseman," Katrina added with a stern voice.

Brom continued his story, upset that he had to finally make these revelations after all this time. "Ichabod was scared out of his wits, but he was alive and well, and he had that handkerchief around his neck. I let him ride off after I threw my pumpkin at him, and that was it."

Brom was exceedingly uncomfortable as his wife looked at him angrily and Van Tassel looked at him disappointedly.

"I thought I was the last human to see him alive…until that day," Brom added.

"Meaning what?" the elder Allen asked.

"He knew Ichabod was dead," Brom answered. "I remember that I firmly believed at that moment that he had seen his body. The only way he could have known about the handkerchief was if he had seen it with his own eyes."

"I don't mean to get in the middle of this town's customs," the elder Allen said. "My son and I have heard about your Headless Horseman legend, too, but could a more plausible possibility be that your marshal did something to this Ichabod Crane, instead of this Headless Horseman?"

Brom was already shaking his head.

"Why not?" Allen asked.

"Because I saw it." Brom's answer made everyone freeze.

"Saw it?" De Graaf asked.

"How do you think I knew Ichabod was taken?" Brom said angrily. "The thing flew past me…I thought it was a waking dream and I…put it all out of my mind."

"But it didn't come after you?" Knickerbocker asked.

Brom shook his head as he looked at his wife. She had a

terrified look on her face.

"It targets only one man at a time," Brom said. "It targeted Ichabod alone. And I was far enough away." He shook his head again. "Again, I put it all out of mind. There was nothing for me to do but...get away and...pretend, to myself especially, that I never saw what I saw."

Everyone was quiet for a moment thinking about Brom's close encounter.

"But you suspected this marshal of having some hand in the event?" the younger Allen asked.

"Yes, but what? I couldn't begin to reason how or why. I simply knew he was someone I personally would keep my distance from," Brom said. "But again, I do believe he saw Ichabod's body."

Katrina turned to Hans. "What was your story about the Marshal?" she asked.

"I saw him trying to bury a pile of bloody clothes in the woods. He pretended he wasn't and moved on from there. I checked those woods later on but there wasn't anything. I'm sure he found another spot."

"And now this Julian Crane person has gone off with this marshal, who used the same story he used with my son's godfather," Allen senior said. "Did not any of you think to warn him to be on the safe side?"

Hans was silent.

"What was I to do?" Brom lashed out. "It was not my business, and the man tried to kill me."

"Who tried to kill you?" Allen asked.

"Julian Crane!"

"Why?"

"He thought I had killed Ichabod Crane."

"Why didn't you tell him what you knew?" Allen asked.

"He had already ridden out with the Marshal," De Graaf defended. "Obviously, Mr. Van Brunt had to recover from his ordeal and be with his family."

"Even if I had a mind to, what would I say?" Brom asked. "Even now, we just have stories, nothing more. These two gentlemen have much more substantial information than us. If the Marshal can't account for your son's godfather, then he could be in serious trouble with the law. Hans and I only had spotted handkerchiefs and piles of bloody clothes—all one man's word against another."

"But what are we going to do about Julian?" Hans asked.

"Yes, what about Mr. Crane?" Knickerbocker asked. "We let him go out there with a man who, let's just be blunt about it, may have killed some innocent men for no cause."

"Is there any possible way to track them?" Old Van Tassel asked De Graaf.

"We already thought about it, Mr. Van Tassel. We don't know exactly where they went. All we know is they went north. They could be anywhere."

"So we're saying that Julian is on his own," Hans said.

"We're saying that Mr. Crane is never coming back alive," Knickerbocker said.

The Storm

"A dark storm will conceal all the dark acts below."

"If you are ever on the Canadian side of the border, look us up and you're more than welcome to our hospitality again," Red said as he and his group waved good-bye to them.

The two men parted with the wagon train not too long after daybreak. The families were heading to towns just north of the Canadian border, but Julian had no idea where the Marshal was taking him.

These were untamed rocky lands, and it was getting rockier as they rode along. In the distance, to his left flank, Julian could see many dark mountains rising from the earth. The sky was overcast, and the mountains looked almost like giant faces watching their every move. He quickly dismissed the feeling as nothing more than the human mind wanting to make order out of the disorder of nature, like seeing shapes in the clouds, but the more he looked, the more he couldn't shake the fact that the mountains did look like faces. Julian turned his eyes away and noticed something else.

There was an eerie glow from behind one of the smaller peaks. He had seen bonfires in the distance before, but this was different. The illumination was muted. It had to be bright enough to be seen from this distance and from behind the mountain, but the light wasn't bright.

"What do you think that glowing is from over there?" he asked the Marshal.

The man glanced at it and stared for a while.

"Who knows? Maybe someone's campfire."

"But the light is strange. I've never seen a fire give off light like that."

"You have Sleepy Hollow scary stories on the brain. It's just a campfire, and it's out of our way so don't ask to investigate it."

Julian thought to himself that perhaps he did pay too much attention to the wagon party's ghost stories last night. But the glow was real, and it was right out of a ghost story. Man hadn't made his mark on these lands and probably never would. It was the kind of land that even the Indians avoided, instead passing down stories to the generations not to trespass. Evil spirits lived here.

"How long will it take to reach there?" Julian asked.

The Marshal seemed to be ignoring him as they rode along. Julian looked ahead and saw it too. The sky was beginning to darken about twenty miles or so ahead.

"What did you ask me?"

"How long will it take to reach there?"

"Well if you had asked me five minutes ago, I would have said one thing, but now I don't know. That looks to be a real bad storm forming up ahead."

Julian looked all around the sky. "Strange how it came up out of nowhere."

"Not strange. Ever seen a tornado? It comes out of nowhere sometimes."

"But that isn't a tornado. It's a storm. A big one, too. Maybe we can outrun it or get out of its path."

"I don't think we can."

"It won't hurt to try."

"Follow me."

Julian kept watching the sky as it transformed from clear to ever-darkening shades of blue. It had the appearance of the entire region being underwater. Then he imagined that the darkening storm clouds were actually a barrier filling up with water draining down from the stars, and at any moment that threshold of clouds would break in a torrent of water and wash them and everything else away.

The Marshal rode on a northeasterly direction and Julian followed. The growing storm hung in the sky as its dark clouds multiplied. It seemed to wait to see where they were heading and then started to move forward again.

"If I didn't know better, I'd say that storm was following after us!"

"Well you do know better!" Marshal yelled back.

They were riding faster across the rocky terrain. It was not even noon and the sky looked more like the hours before sunset and looking into the coming storm it looked as dark as night. Julian looked directly above his head and suddenly felt his entire body levitating into sky.

"No!" he yelled out realizing he had been thrown.

Caleb Williams' body arched and his head hung as he landed back down to the ground. Julian crashed to the ground hard.

The Marshal was riding between two hills and glanced back. He stopped his horse. Julian was gone! He pulled his gun as a look of anger swept across his face. The young Crane probably thought he could get away under the cover of the storm without anyone being able to trace his tracks. Marshal grinned. No one knew this area better than he. The Marshal turned his horse around and rode back hard.

Julian picked himself up and was thankful he landed on dirt rather than rocks. He slowly walked to his horse with his hands open. "Whoa, Caleb Williams. Stay calm." He grabbed the reins.

What startled my horse?

His horse had been startled before but had never thrown him from his back.

Something smacked the lower part of right boot. Julian stood still. It was not his imagination as something hit him again. He looked down and saw both of his feet were standing on a slithering shape.

Julian jumped back and Caleb Williams almost leapt up again. Julian drew on the black snake as it crawled not away, but towards them! As he aimed at the reptile, his eyes could see a new shape coming at him from the corner of his eye. The shot hit the snake point-blank and Julian aimed his gun at the shape that was taking form, though his gun was empty.

Marshal stood in front of him.

"That wasn't the smartest thing I ever saw a lawman do. I could have shot you," Julian scolded.

"If I knew you had a gun in your hand, I wouldn't have done what I did, obviously," the Marshal said. "I didn't know what happened to you. You disappeared."

Julian returned his gun to his holster. "A snake startled my horse and threw me."

"This snake." The Marshal picked something up from the ground with the tip of his boot.

Julian leaned closer and saw that the snake was much larger than he thought.

"Can't say I ever saw a rattlesnake like this one before," Marshal said. "I hate to imagine what would have happened if it bit your horse or you."

Julian looked up at the sky. "Let's move and hope we don't see any others."

Marshal looked up the sky too. "We may have to find shelter sooner rather than later."

Julian sighed. "There's not much here. The sky is turning black so fast. I've never seen a storm move in this quick."

"We'll have to ride faster."

Julian pulled his horse along to follow Marshal, but now he felt nervous about the terrain at their feet. Every tiny shadow brought on anxiety in him.

The Marshal mounted his horse with one hand and secretly placed his gun back in his holster. Julian also got back on his horse and then quickly, and blindly, reloaded his gun.

The men rode their horses as quickly as the horses could take along the uneven, jagged terrain. The trees and brush became scarcer. The dirt turned sandy as they rode. The first bolt of lightning flashed in the distance. There was a rolling rumble and three seconds later, the thunder exploded, spooking the horses.

Marshal quickened the pace as they raced the horses. Another sound of thunder, then another exploded. The dark clouds had already overtaken them, and then the rain started to pour. It was coming down so hard that they knew they'd soon have to dismount again. There were several large trees in easy distance, but taking refuge under one of them could be a death trap. Lightning liked striking tall things in the middle of emptiness.

As they had thought, lightning struck a tree in the distance and shattered it in half, causing the entire thing to catch on fire.

The men were now fighting their horses to push on. The frequent lightning and louder and louder thunder was panicking the animals. Marshal raised his hand, stopped his horse, and jumped down. Julian did the same. At any moment, the horses would throw them.

Marshal led his horse by the reins and calmly walked forward, with a following Julian. The rain was fierce, the lightning never-ending and thunder deafening. But there seemed no place to take shelter.

They also faced a new danger. First it was only splashes as their feet hit new puddles along the ground, but now the ground was turning into its own river, and causing the men to almost slip several times. The only saving grace for them was that they were steadily moving up to higher ground, and the terrain was rocky enough to allow the water to flow downward and into crevasses away from them. However, with this downpour, gravity wouldn't be able to rescue them or their horses from the floodwaters, especially as the rain intensified all around them. They weren't at the top yet so it was also possible that all of them could be washed down the mountainous land at any time. There was no indication that this storm would let up soon, just the opposite.

One of the lightning strikes illuminated the entire area with such a brightness that both Julian and his horse jumped. He noticed a large stone in the floodwater around them.

Maybe I can pick it up, sneak up behind the Marshal, and bash his skull in. Julian dismissed the thought for the moment. *Good people don't behave that way.*

Marshal suddenly began in a different direction. At this point, Julian couldn't see anything other than the Marshal's back with the lack of natural light and the blinding rain. The Marshal then seemed to disappear into pitch-black and then the rain stopped.

"I'll try to start a fire," Marshal called out. They were in a cave. "Not that I have any chance whatsoever of succeeding. At least we're out of the rain and lightning."

Julian was about to squeeze the excess water out of his clothes but thought to himself, why bother? He was drenched and in a moment, he was going to be drenched and freezing. He ran his hand over Caleb William's forehead and then patted him a few times.

"Marshal, we're never going to be able to make a fire in this dampness—"

A fire lit up, and the image of the Marshal was before him. He held in his hand what seemed to be a torch.

Eek! Eek! Eek!

An explosion of tiny squeaks startled Julian and echoed all around them. A flapping swarm enveloped the Marshal as the frightened bats flew out of the cave. Julian turned his head away as he covered Caleb Williams with his body until the sounds were gone.

"That's an unsettling experience that I hope to never have again," Julian said.

"Being swarmed by hundreds of bats? It's nothing. Think of them as funny-faced birds with leathery wings. They're more scared of us than anything. And there's no such thing as vampires out to get your blood."

Marshal lifted the burning, rolled-up newspaper high above his head. Julian kept trying to figure how Marshal could start a fire in all this dampness as the men inspected the cave. "Let's keep the horses near the entrance. We have to figure out a way to secure them without them being able to run off. If they do, we may never find them again."

"I'll do that."

Marshal moved quickly to find any kind of possible tinder in the cave before the newspaper burnt away. Julian walked to the mouth of the cave, and the rain continued to pour down with no less intensity. The entire sky was black except for the lightning strikes that lit it up like it was high noon. He used rope from his saddle pack to create a makeshift fence across the cave entrance and weighted their reins to the ground with as many large stones as he could find. He prayed it would keep the horses inside.

He stuck his head outside for a moment. The rain poured down with such ferocity that he had to pull himself back in. The storm settled on its spot, which was right above them. It made Julian angry, and he stepped back into the rain and forced his head to look up at it. The entire ground shook with a rumble of thunder and then three bolts of lightning shot down almost simultaneously, with the last one no more than twenty feet away. Julian gave up on his defiance. They would be prisoners of the cave until the storm decided to let them go.

The cave was illuminated with the glow of a roaring

flame. Julian walked back inside and saw the Marshal kneeling down in front of it, rubbing his hands. Julian joined him. Based on the material he used to make the fire, it looked like the cave had human visitors before, and hopefully it had no non-human visitors now.

At some point in the night—or was it still daytime—the thunder cracked so loud that the cave shook. Julian jumped up to check on the horses. Marshal got up several times himself to walk to the cave entrance, out of sight, to see about the rain.

Julian got his coffee kit from his saddle pack to make coffee for both of them. That's all they cared for at moment. It was all about the waiting now.

"Know any good stories?" Julian asked as he nursed his now-cold tin of coffee. "I'd even settle for a few ghost stories."

Marshal managed to smile. "I have always found real life to be scary enough."

"Then tell me about my uncle to pass the time."

Marshal smiled. "Sure." He got comfortable and lit his cigar with the fire. "Where should I start? Oh, how about at the beginning. I met Ichabod…"

As the Marshal told the story, Julian did let his mind wander about his uncle Ichabod. Most of what he knew of the man was the experiences and memories of others. His own late father, Ichabod's brother, never spoke of him, and neither did his mother. There was no bad blood between them. They had all simply lost touch with one another.

The storm raged on, and if it had been daylight before, it was nighttime now. The lightning became less frequent and the thunder less deafening as Marshal talked about

Ichabod Crane. Julian got up a few times to check on the horses, while the Marshal got up a few times to check on the storm.

Julian got up a final time to go outside to empty his bladder before turning in. The storm seemed to finally be moving on. He could visibly see the dark clouds drift off in the night sky. He walked back through the cave entrance and wanted to check on his horse and supplies. Hopefully, nothing fell off in the storm. Caleb Williams was quiet as a mouse, unlike the Marshal's horse, which was still restless despite the storm seemingly moving on. It took Julian moments to check and re-check through his saddle pack, then his weapon.

All his ammunition in his pack was gone.

Psycho

"That is what I am!"

Julian stood there in the dark. In the future, he supposed they would make guns that could shoot more than one bullet at a time, but today was not that future. He had one bullet in his gun and that was it. He had the image of him walking back in to the fire and the Marshal gut-shooting him as he did to Frenchie. He had the image of lying on the ground trying to sleep and the Marshal killing him that way, with a bullet to the head. His mind raced with all the ways his life could end in this cave at the hands of the Marshal. "Don't play with danger," his father had told him.

"Marshal Crane, do you want any more coffee before I dump out the pot?"

Julian walked back at the fire. "No, that's it for me tonight."

Marshal dumped it out in a corner of the cave. "It's probably best if we sleep in shifts. It isn't only humans who seek caves out for shelter. Any number of animals could run in here or attack the horses."

"I'll take first watch then. I can barely sleep as it is," Julian said in truth.

"Can't say I ever had that problem." Marshal situated himself on his bedroll next to the fire. "Wake me in four hours."

Julian sat down. "Four hours it is."

Julian never did wake him, but somehow Marshal woke on his own almost exactly four hours later. The rain had started again, but this time it was a light drizzle. Julian lay down and the Marshal warmed his hands by the fire again.

He was on his side with his head facing the Marshal. His head rested on his hands, and he only half-closed his eyes.

Marshal spent his four hours scratching himself, playing a card game, and, at one point in the night, added more brush from the cave into the fire. Then he stood up tall and put his hand on the belt of his holster. Julian watched carefully as the Marshal stood there with his head bowed and eyes closed.

What was he doing?

The horses suddenly went wild, and Julian could hear growls of some animal.

With no warning, the Marshal shot his gun!

Julian jumped up from his sleeping spot. All he heard were the yelps of some canine. Marshal ran to the cave entrance with Julian following. They could see the coyotes run away across the plain—a pack of them.

Neither man could sleep. Marshal played his card game on the ground and Julian wrote in his journal.

The night sky lit up with occasional lightning, and then it went pitch black again. When the lightning flashed again, they could see the shapes of the watching coyotes. There were at least a dozen of them spread out in front of the cave ten yards away or more. It was as if they purposely wanted to ensure there was no way the men could slip away.

A crack of thunder startled everyone, and the coyotes took off running. The sky lit up again and they saw the coyotes running back to their positions in the area in front of the cave. The animals took to growling at them from the distance.

Two of the coyotes to the furthest left waited, with one of them hiding behind a small boulder. To their furthest right was a large coyote, his growls were especially menacing. The other coyotes were scattered around between at different distances.

Both men watched them to see if there was any clue as to which one might be the alpha of the pack. While all the others were taking turns growling at the men, and some even crawled forward a few paces, there was one in the center that remained quiet, lying close to the ground. All they could see were its glistening eyes locked in on them. Maybe it thought it was a snake as it crawled forward a bit more as the other made more noise with their growling. The animals knew they had a gun, but rather than run away, these coyotes were unnaturally aggressive. Julian thought to himself how everything about this land was black and venal. If they stayed long enough, crazed insects would be next to attack them.

"You should shoot a couple of them," Julian said. "I'm sure that will teach them, and they'll at least stay further away from the cave."

The Marshal loaded and fired his pistol once.

The closest animal to them jumped up and fell back to the ground dead. The other coyotes raced away as if they were on fire. There was no pause between another of their fellow coyotes collapsing dead to the ground. The others disappeared into the night. The second shot from the Marshal's rifle still seemed to echo.

"That should keep the devils away for the night," Marshal said.

The men rode out at sunrise.

"Where did this Legend of Sleepy Hollow come from?" Julian asked.

"It's something about the place, whether you believe in spirits or not. It casts a spell on people, like a witching power, makes them live in…what was the phrase I was told? 'Continual reverie,'" Marshall replied. "Whites say the place was bewitched by some German doctor at the precolonial days of the town. Indians say it was an old chief, part prophet, part wizard.

"Despite my personal dealings with them, I can honestly say the people of Sleepy Hollow are a good people."

The Marshal started to slow his horse. "That's it exactly. Good people deserving of protection."

The Marshal had a wild look in his eyes, but in a moment it was gone, and he began riding along again.

"When will we get to my uncle's place?"

"Soon. We'll be there by night fall."

"What's the name of this town he's in?"

"It's called the Junction."

"Is it on the American side or the Canadian side?"

"American side."

"My uncle was planning on moving south not north."

"Well he clearly changed his mind if that's where he resides today."

Julian stopped his horse this time and glared at Marshal.

"What's wrong with you?" Marshal asked.

"You forgot to do something, Marshal."

"What's that?"

"Reload your guns after you shot that coyote."

"No need. My second rifle is always ready, and I can reload a gun in less than five seconds."

"Let's see that in action."

Julian yelled at Caleb Williams at the top of his lungs. The horse bolted forward toward some nearby trees. The Marshal was caught off guard and at first reached for his rifle, then for his ammo. It was too late. Julian reached the trees and took position behind them.

Marshal laughed. "You caught me there. I guess I'm not as fast as my conceit had me believe."

"Did you kill my uncle?" Julian yelled at him.

Marshal didn't answer for a moment. "What a crazy thing to say! I'm taking you to him, aren't I?"

"The only crazy thing here is you! My uncle wouldn't move out here! There's nothing out here but deranged animals! A perfect place for you! It was you who killed my uncle Ichabod! You foul murderer!"

"I didn't kill—"

"Who didn't you kill, Marshal? My uncle? Frenchie? Who knows how many others? I saw you kill Frenchie in cold blood. I know you're leading me into the middle of nowhere so you can do to me what you did to them."

"Now settle down, Marshal Crane. You've gotten your mind twisted up and believing all kinds of things that ain't true. I'm taking you to your uncle right now. This is what you wanted. And then I'm going to return to my post."

"You're not returning to any post as a U.S. Marshal, you murderer!"

"Shut up! Shut up! Shut up! Shut up!" The wildness was back in his eyes. He kicked at his horse and raced towards Julian.

Julian didn't wait. He turned Caleb Williams and was off.

Marshal chased Julian for miles. They rode away from the mountains into deeper forest. As Julian neared a new thicker patch of trees, Marshal knew he had only one chance and grabbed his rifle to shoot.

Julian knew what he was going to do and was already looking back. He aimed and shot his only bullet. Marshal was thrown clear as his horse crashed to the ground. Julian stopped his horse and road to cover behind the largest tree he could see.

Marshal picked himself off the ground and dusted himself off.

"That was some fine shooting, Marshal Crane!"

His horse looked up at him with its broken body, dying. "Fine shooting!" He aimed his rifle and shot the horse in the head.

Marshal sat down on the ground to compose himself. He was breathing hard, abnormally fast.

"Marshal Crane, you have to understand, I did it all for the good people of Sleepy Hollow. The Headless Horseman is the commander-in-chief of all the powers of the night. Its power is beyond your imagination. You can't stop it, but I entered into a pact with it. I was able to gain influence over it. You know how? I found its head. Yes, me! It would leave the Hollow and its region alone. I moved it here, and I entered into a pact to provide it victims. It would stay here, away from the Hollow, and I'd provide it fresh victims."

Marshal stood to his feet again and leaned down to the saddle pack on his dead horse.

"For ten years, no one has seen the Horseman anywhere in the Hollow. I am the one responsible for that, responsible for them being able to live and grow as a town, soon a real city.

"Frenchie stumbled onto what I was doing, and I had to silence him. This is bigger than one man, two men. Don't you see that, Marshal Crane? The Horseman is too powerful. I brought it to this place, and it made it its base. I didn't even have to do anything. The land just transformed into its domain. The plants, animals, insects, the trees, grass, the atmosphere all around. It is becoming more powerful every day, and I have to keep the victims coming so that the pact will not be broken."

"Where does the Horseman live, Marshal?" Julian yelled out.

"Two miles that way." The Marshal pointed northwest. "I told you that I was going to take you to your uncle. The Horsemen killed him, not me. And it took him to its lair, like it does with all its victims. So many of them. It started its quest long before me. I don't think it came to being from the War. I believe it was here long before us, maybe before the Indians, too."

Marshal started to laugh hysterically. The laughter didn't stop and became more bizarre.

"Marshal Crane, you have no more bullets," he mocked.

"How many men have you killed? How many men have you done the same to as you did to Frenchie, or how you're trying to do to me now? How much blood do you have on your hands? How much Hollow blood?"

Julian had already dismounted from his horse and stood near a large tree for cover, but Marshal was marching to him.

"My intention was to take you to the Horseman too, Marshal Crane. It would have taken you too. You would have become part of its Devil's Pumpkin Patch forever." He started to cackle. "Ichabod Crane and Julian Crane together. I told you I would reunite both of you. I did not lie."

"You mad murderer!" Julian shouted back.

Marshal was only a few yards from him.

"How can I be a mad murderer, Marshal Crane? There is no such thing as the Headless Horseman. You said so yourself." He started to laugh again, but suddenly stopped. "I'm going to kill you and take you to him. You and your uncle will be together in the same dirt."

Marshal stepped forward a few paces with his rifle in hand—he had reloaded it while he had been talking and laughing. Julian came out from behind the tree to face the man. Marshal smiled as he raised his rifle to shoot.

Julian spun around in a circle, whipping his arm around.

Twenty years ago in his Connecticut town, he and his boyhood friends used to invent games to play. The things frontier boys would do to make the day go by. Once, they used an old Indian bow to shoot real arrows to knock apples off each other's heads. Another was climbing a thirty-foot tree, scurrying up with hands, feet, forearms, and using even fingernails to claw into the bark. It was more dangerous climbing down though, than climbing up. But the game with the axes—take an ax, spin around and around, and see who could throw it the furthest. The ax flew through the air as another boy, a fellow member of the gang, appeared in the field from nowhere. The ax's blade arched down to his head. The boys watched helplessly, and their mouths were open so wide, screaming in horror, but there were no sounds that came out, as if any amount of screaming could make reality turn into a bad dream. Nothing that could make time skip back so that they would not do what they did.

The Marshal looked like he did. He looked back at Julian like that in frozen shock, with his eyes bulging and mouth wide open. The tomahawk was buried in his face, from forehead to the end of his nose, a vertical spout of red showering forth. Marshal Damian Marshall fell backwards to the ground, dead.

Part III
The Hessian

Ride! Across the Bridge From Hell!

"As the pumpkin flies!"

He was tired. So close but still very far away from his ultimate objective.

A fair-haired man sat at the table alone staring at his alcohol-filled glass. His cowboy hat was set on the table next to the glass, and despite the rowdiness of the pub, he was so deep in thought that everything going on around him was tuned out.

The life of a bounty hunter was one of danger and profit. It attracted a certain type who thrived on the chase, the long periods of loneliness and boredom on the trail, and then the rush of the capture. But there had to be a bounty. There had to be money waiting at the end of the hunt, or no matter how much the man thrived on that danger he would not be interested if there was no reward waiting. No one cared about justice, the system of law and order, innocence or guilt. They wanted a solid payday. It was the only motivation, not revenge like him.

Shaunessy had been many places along the Atlantic Seaboard, many towns, and came across many different men in his search. They said he had even been to foreign lands beyond his native Europe where the people spoke languages no one had ever heard, except the wealthy explorer who had the means to go. He had been many places, and all because of a singular event that had occurred in the New York town of Sleepy Hollow.

He had never heard of the place. He had not heard of many towns in America, why should this one be special? But it was special. It was the town that his father had been "taken." That was the queer term they had for it. His father was taken by the Headless Horseman of Sleepy Hollow. Was it a ghost? An earthbound devil? Some other creature of the night? No one could tell him with any certainty, other than to tell him it reigned above all other horrors of the night.

He was after the ultimate bounty, after this thing, but after all his years of preparing, he had reached the end of his means.

That's what he lacked—the money. He didn't have the means to see his hunt to the end. He had the desire, born from his vengeful hatred. He had his "secret weapon" to use against it, but no more. He lacked the means to put everything together in a final package to make it happen. As he sat at the table, he realized he didn't know what that package should be, except to know he didn't have it. He had met all the men he knew that could help him succeed in his supernatural hunt, but they had no more regard for him and his goals than they did for a nameless chicken crossing the road. He didn't have the means, but he was taunted in knowing that the means were within his reach. Simply, he had no ability to grab it.

Another man walked up to the table. Morgan was an irritable, easily provoked, and fidgety man, but he was also an exceptional gunman. He could be annoying, but today Shaunessy found his company welcoming.

"I never met an Irishman who drinks as little as you." Morgan sat down in the chair next to him. "There's no point getting sad about it. Unless you can make it worth everyone's time and expense, I don't see what else can be done but go home."

"I have to find a way. I must. The thing killed my father."

"Shaunessy, I'm going to say this to you, not to be mean, but I don't care. Nobody does. You care because you're supposed to. But the rest of us don't. If I were in your place, then I'd be doing the exact same thing as you, but I wouldn't expect you to care one bit. You gotta come up with a worthy incentive or it ends. I'm sorry."

Morgan watched the distress on Shaunessy's face.

"Will you stick around a few more days?" Shaunessy asked.

"Only a day or two. I have to eat same as the next man."

"That's fair."

Morgan had nothing else to add.

"I suppose I have to pray for an answer," Shaunessy said.

"Or pray for someone to come along and give you a bunch of money so you can pay people. That's an incentive I can get behind. Revenge for you, and money for the rest. You'll need more than just two for sure. That would work."

"If only there was someone in Sleepy Hollow who could finance the hunt."

"Have you tried? Have you even been to Sleepy Hollow yet?"

"No."

"Then that's what you should do. I can't go with you, but you should go and see what you can make happen. That's what you should do. Pray for that, Irishman."

From the back of Caleb Williams, Julian watched the violent sight from the hill. The coyotes had returned in force, but this time Marshal wouldn't be shooting at them or anything else ever again. The beasts were fighting amongst themselves—growling, biting, pushing, and scratching—for the body of the madman. Like the black vultures days before, these beasts were also a foreboding black in appearance that he could now see in the daylight. They, too, had taken to dragging the corpse away as they feasted. Like the black vultures, their group behavior was unlike he had ever seen before. Julian had to get away from this unnatural place.

He could see the glint of his tomahawk's blade protruding from the Marshal's fleshless skull. The tomahawk was a gift from one of the Indian braves General Washington had introduced him to as a boy-soldier in the Continental Army. He was so proud of the weapon because unlike a regular man's musket, he could easily brandish it. The brave told him to keep it with him at all times "in battle" and it would protect his life. The brave was right. Julian had a special pocket in his coat made for it, and he always had his coat. He had never used it until today. He watched with sadness as the weapon was dragged away into oblivion along with the Marshal's corpse by the coyotes. He knew he would never see it again.

Julian was disgusted with himself for watching the carnage for so long. As he rode out, he realized why. He wanted no part in the supernatural. It was an easy thing to hunt a man, but an apparition? He still wondered if he believed in the thing. There were plenty of people who did and would swear on a bible about its existence. He just wasn't sure if he was such a person yet.

Marshal told him two miles due northwest, so that is where he went.

Julian realized that he was heading towards where he had seen the glowing behind the mountain before the storm came. He was sure he had covered at least five miles already but there was nothing but locust trees, and the mountains were still in the distance off to the side. He heard the rushing flow of water and slowly rode towards it. There he found a river with dark opaque waters. Instinctively, he rode Caleb Williams over to its bank for him to get a drink. The horse sniffed the water and then jerked its head up and turned away. That was a first—his horse refusing water. Julian looked down at it and decided he didn't want it either.

He noticed an old-looking bridge wide enough for two horses to ride side-by side. As he neared it, he realized that he was mistaken. It looked brand-new, but its entire structure was entangled with unsightly vines and brush. He remembered what the old man on the wagon train said about the Horseman's power. Assuming the Marshal told him the truth and this was the Horseman's domain, its power would only exist on the other side of the bridge, on the other side of this dark river. However, he remembered the other thing the old man said: the apparition could throw its deadly pumpkin projectile well past the river's boundary.

Julian had used pumpkins in his Sleepy Hollow investigation to be prankish and provocative. But he didn't find anything amusing about them now. He noticed that the ground across the river was covered thick with pumpkins, with smaller ones close to the water and increasingly larger away from the riverbank.

He took a deep breath. "Caleb Williams, let's cross the bridge."

Caleb Williams was gripped with a terrified hysteria as it sprinted faster than its legs had ever done before. Julian hung onto him with all his might until somehow the reins broke. Then he frantically wrapped his arms around his horse's neck to stay on. The crushing fear had turned Julian's face pale as he fought the impulse to look back. He mustn't, he kept repeating to himself, yelling to himself. If he looked back, it would get him. But he was losing the battle not to do so.

They reached it! They were upon the bridge and about to cross. He relented and looked back. The pumpkin projectile filled his entire view as it came hurtling at his face. He jerked his head to the side, but the impact smacked his jawbone, threw him from the horse, and smashed him into the bridge itself with a deafening thud.

A terrified Caleb Williams continued across, picking up speed rather than slowing for his master. Julian, empowered by sheer adrenaline alone, rose up and ran across the bridge too, oblivious to his pain or injuries, as he was running for his life. Julian made it across and followed the dust trail left behind by his no longer visible fleeing horse. He glimpsed back across the river as he sprinted over the hills.

Through a haunting mist, the Headless Horseman sat on its black horse of death. Every pumpkin on its islet domain was glowing.

Hollow Blood (Book One of the Sleepy Hollow Horrors) concludes in *The Devil's Patch* (Book Two).

Thank you for reading!

Dear Reader,

I hope you enjoyed **Hollow Blood** (Sleepy Hollow Horrors, Book 1).

<u>Can You Write Me a Review?</u>

If you enjoyed **Hollow Blood**, I'd greatly appreciate a review on one or more of the following sites:

amazon BARNES&NOBLE BOOKSELLERS kobo

goodreads iBooks

Reviews are the best way for readers to discover good books. My writer's motto is simple: "Readers Rule!" Thanks so much.

Always writing,

Austin Dragon

ABOUT THE AUTHOR

Austin Dragon is the author of the *After Eden* **Series**, including the *After Eden: Tek-Fall* mini-series, the classic *Sleepy Hollow Horrors*, and the upcoming cyberpunk detective series, *Liquid Cool*. He is a native New Yorker, but has called Los Angeles, California home for the last twenty years. Words to describe him, in no particular order: U.S. Army; English teacher; one-time resident of Paris; political junkie; movie buff; campaign manager and staffer of presidential and gubernatorial campaigns; Fortune 500 corporate recruiter; renaissance man; dreamer.

He is currently working on new books and series in mystery, fantasy, YA dystopia, classic horror, and more science fiction!

Connect with Austin on social media at:

Website and blog: http://www.austindragon.com

Twitter: https://twitter.com/Austin_Dragon

Pinterest: http://www.pinterest.com/austindragon

Google+: https://google.com/+AustinDragonAuthor

Goodreads: https://www.goodreads.com/ADragon

Other books by Austin Dragon

See all my books at: http://www.austindragon.com/books-of-author-austin-dragon/

Continue the Adventure!

Join my **VIP Readers' Club** through my website for all the latest announcements, upcoming book releases, and events; behind-the-scenes and sneak peeks; contests and special offers—including free ebooks and excerpts! Visit http://www.austindragon.com/be_a_vip/ to get started.

Made in the USA
Columbia, SC
07 May 2025